Harry Saves
the World

Harry Saves the World

GARY ALEXANDER

Encircle Publications, LLC
Farmington, Maine U.S.A.

CHAPTER 1

Near midnight, a Focke-Wulf Fw 200 Condor cruised low over the Rio Tejo, banking steeply as it approached the city. Two of its four 9-cylinder, 875-horsepower Pratt & Whitney Hornet radial engines were shut down to avoid attention from the ground. Lapis lazuli twilight lined the horizon. It went unappreciated by the sole passenger, a failed artist.

The Condor carried a light load, so 50-percent power was more than ample. It was a modern aircraft, an all-metal monoplane designed as an airliner that could hold as many as 26 passengers in two cabins, but this aircraft was configured luxuriously for only the one it now carried, plus one attendant. For security reasons, the passenger's personal pilot flew without a copilot.

The passenger sat at a folding table of his design. A clock, altimeter and airspeed indicator were on a bulkhead directly ahead of him. Why these instruments were important to the illustrious passenger was anybody's guess, and nobody dared ask him. The man was suspicious of everyone and everything. Undue attention to him and to his personal habits placed one in peril.

As the pilot headed landward, Lisbon came into view. The passenger stared out his window in amazement at lights as far as he could see. The City of Seven Hills was now the City of Light, he thought. Paris was blacked out, as were most European cities, largely his doing.

Neutrality was frustrating, he thought sourly. Maddening. If he

1

could only persuade Francisco Franco to bring Spain into the war, Portugal's Antonio Salazar would have to follow. But that was for another day.

The flight attendant, a uniformed SS officer, approached the passenger nervously, hoping that he didn't notice that he was holding his breath. No one dared inform the great man that he often made the cabin smell like a sewer.

"We are going to be landing momentarily, *mein Führer*."

"Yes yes," Hitler said, waving him away.

Despite often opting for air travel instead or rail for sake of efficiency, Adolf Hitler disliked flying. It made him sweaty and nervous, and exacerbated his flatulence, which was virtually uncontrollable in any event.

Der Fartenführer, some whispered, aware that they faced a death sentence if overheard.

The pilot put down the landing gear and lowered the flaps to full extension. The hydraulic noise directly underneath made the *Führer* fidget. It did not improve his mood.

Adolf Hitler was making this trip against his better judgment. France was now under Reich protection and the English were next to fall. His vision was being realized and there was so much to do.

After Reichsmarschall Hermann Göring's Luftwaffe cleansed the skies of the Royal Air Force, Hitler could turn his attention to Operation Sea Lion, the invasion of Great Britain. He was already thinking ahead how to best use Englishmen as slave labor in Germany's factories and mines. They were ethnically superior to the Slavs and Poles, so the Reich could extract much more benefit from them as they were being worked to death.

The architects of this farfetched scheme in Lisbon had begged him to interrupt his schedule to see this "secret weapon" in person. Large numbers of the *Engländer* enemy will die horrible deaths and the lives of the Fatherland's troops would be spared if the invasion can be postponed, they promised.

Hitler was intrigued, but wary. German scientists had been working in the same direction at home, with little success.

The proponents argued that if the secret weapon worked, Reich forces could step ashore in England without the loss of a single life and to the intoxicating aroma of rotting corpses. A proposal to counterfeit the England pound note and drop them all over the country to cause hyperinflation and destabilize the economy would also be unnecessary.

A man who knew his history, Adolf Hitler would be the first invader to step on British soil since William the Conqueror in 1066. After this came to pass, he would be free to turn his attention eastward, to the eradication of the Bolsheviks.

In many respects, the *Führer* was hidebound. He firmly believed that wars were won by armies crushing the opponents on the ground. In the nightmarish trenches of the Great War, he had won the Iron Cross, First Class in 1918. Corporal Adolf Hitler had been wounded and also gassed, temporarily blinded by the fumes. He vowed to avenge that war's humiliating outcome.

Days earlier, he had toured Paris and authored an armistice with the French at Compiègne, where the mortifying 1918 armistice was signed. The shoe was on the other foot this time! Hitler then ordered the site destroyed and the trolley in which the signing was done moved to Berlin.

These scientists and their secret weapon had better be the genuine goods, he thought. He had neither time nor patience for folly.

Lisbon's Portela Airport was under construction, not due to officially open until 1942, in over two years, but one runway was sufficiently completed, made available for special visitors. Its lights came on seconds before the Focke-Wulf touched down.

In the event they had been observed, the markings on the Führer's airplane had been painted over with Switzerland's flag, a white cross on a red background. The minute they arrived back home, workers would make the swastika reappear.

Before it rolled to a complete stop and its engines had been shut down, a fuel truck pulled up on one side and a Mercedes W142 sedan on the other. Hitler walked down steps where he was greeted by a senior German Embassy attaché (i.e. Lisbon SS chief) who clicked his heels and thrust a Nazi salute.

"I am Horst Wessel. It is the greatest of honors, *mein Führer.*"

Jut-jawed, cold blue eyes, cornflower hair; if there was such a thing as being *too* Aryan, he was it, Hitler thought. Named Horst Wessel? Same as the famed National Socialist hero and martyr, that was quite a coincidence. *The Horst Wessel Song* was the Reich's sacred anthem.

Hitler was tired after the long flight. He unenthusiastically returned the salute and got into the Mercedes. After ensuring that the rear window curtains were down, the driver hurriedly closed the doors.

When they were underway, Hitler said, "Prime Minister Salazar doesn't know what you are doing or that I am here?"

"No, *mein Führer.*"

"Anybody? The police, anybody?"

"The Portuguese security police, the PVDE, have made inquiries about activities at this location."

"And?"

"They have been paid to be forgetful and to keep snoopers at a distance. This facility is under strict German control."

"I am told that the scientist who is in charge of developing this weapon is a Jew and that Nordic scientists and technicians are under his direction, taking all instructions from this Jew."

The attaché dreaded this question. Talking fast, Horst Wessel said, "This is true and while vermin, the *Juden* can be brilliant scientists. His wife, children, parents, and every close relative and friend have been relocated to our camps, *mein Führer*. Devotion to the project and loyalty to the Fatherland is assured."

"All relatives and all others close to him?"

Hitler had asked these questions innumerable times before departing Berlin. He was known for repeating questions in the hope of tripping somebody up.

"Every one we could find, *mein Führer*. Approximately two hundred of them."

"Round up friends and acquaintances of *them*. How many are there, do you estimate?"

"A thousand at the least," Wessel said, guessing.

"Do it."

"I will have it done immediately."

"They will enjoy the fresh air and robust health of the Polish countryside."

Wessel looked at him. Adolf Hitler had a made a joke? But he wasn't smiling.

Should he laugh? Horst Wessel didn't know. He *did* know that the other lead scientist on the project, also a Jew, was gone, presumably dead. He had been accidently exposed to the deadly compound during an earlier stage of development, showing horrific symptoms, burning up with fever. Before he could be disposed of—as were other workers that unfortunate—he escaped, saying that he was going into the Rio Tejo to cool off. Stupidly, this was permitted by a dull-witted SS corporal on guard duty, a man who paid dearly for his negligence.

The escapee hadn't been seen since. Horst Wessel prayed to the God he didn't believe in that Hitler knew nothing of the second Jew scientist and didn't demand to see them both.

"I have been told vague technical things, what this poison can do. It isn't a gas, is it?"

"Oh no, *mein Führer*. We were informed of your prohibition of poison gas. We follow your orders explicitly."

"I personally know of mustard gas from the last war. If we gas them, they will gas us. The RAF will drop canisters all over the Reich. I will not approve the use of poison gas."

"I can assure you, *mein Führer*, it is not a gas. It is like nothing the world has ever seen. If it is used, there will be no pilots left to fly Royal Air Force planes. Technical experts can explain it much better than I."

Hitler didn't reply.

During the ride, Hitler peeked out his window. Well-dressed people were out and about, enjoying pastries and drinks in cafés. There was no shortage of cars on the streets either. Poorly dressed people were on the sidewalks too. Refugees, he thought. Refugees who had fled *him*. They were all consuming food, liquor, gasoline and electricity that rightfully belonged to the Third Reich. They needed to be rounded up and shot, each and every one of them.

When he slept the best, Adolf Hitler dreamt of turbulent streams of blood.

The Mercedes slowed and turned. It drove *thump-thump-thump* along a heavy wooden pier.

"We are almost there, *mein Führer*."

"Do not tell me where we are," Hitler shrieked. "I do not want to hear where we are. You are not here, I am not here. This *here* does not exist."

"Of course, *mein Führer*. Of course not," Wessel said, tightening his sphincter, looking at him and nodding furiously.

The savior of Aryan civilization was dressed in a double-breasted suit and a hat that rode low, mufti that did not conceal a unique moustache and cold, bulging eyes. Seated close enough to *touch* Adolf Hitler, the messiah of civilization, Horst Wessel was simultaneously euphoric and terrified.

He was reminded of a 1936 speech given by Dr. Joseph Goebbels, the Reich's Minister of Public Enlightenment and Propaganda, remembering one passage verbatim. "Germany has been transformed into a great house of the Lord where the *Führer* as our mediator stands before the throne of God."

He was not alone in his reverence. Robert Ley, head of the German Labor Front, said, "We believe on this earth in Adolf Hitler alone! We believe in National Socialism as the creed which is the sole source of grace!"

And then there was the visionary Reinhard Heydrich, who in 1935 said, "You will see the day ten years from now when Adolf Hitler will occupy precisely the same position that Jesus Christ has now."

Hitler himself had proclaimed, "Who says I am not under the special protection of God?"

Horst Wessel was clammy, seeing stars. He did not believe that the man beside him was being immodest. Nor had the others embellished. He was sitting with a deity!

Feeling a glow beside him, a luminosity (and a halo?), he dared not look. On the verge of swooning, Horst Wessel said, "You are so right, *mein Führer.*"

Hitler didn't answer. This was Reinhard Heydrich's brainstorm, a proposition Reinhard had sold to his superior, Heinrich Himmler. They claimed it was a project to stunningly shorten the war. Further, it was being established in a neutral country that would not be threatened by British air raids.

This was something they had found in some technical magazine, Hitler initially thought. Possibly a child's comic book. Those two did have creative imaginations. Some of their ideas were absurd. For instance, shipping all European Jews to Madagascar, just them and the savages. But it was just an island that could receive a fraction of the total number. Their hearts were in the right place, he felt, but their heads were in the clouds.

This secret-weapon notion was fantastical, yes, but if by some slim chance it came to fruition the result could be magnificent.

Continuation of the project awaited Hitler's approval and the appropriation of funds needed to continue, payment accepted by the principals only in precious gold. Payment in any currency would raise suspicions.

Show me something tangible, or enough was enough, Hitler had told Heydrich. Produce the goods or we move on to the more tangible projects.

Reinhard was confident he could. Hitler agreed on this disruptive junket on the condition that he came alone, not subject to persuasion or influence. The most powerful man on the planet could make up his own mind.

Adolf Hitler especially liked and admired Reinhard Heydrich, an individual he thought of as a man with an iron heart. To *SS-Obergrupperführer* Heydrich, murder was merely a tool for the greater good of the Reich, unencumbered by weakling notions of right and wrong. To kill on behalf of National Socialist Germany was sanitation, cleansing, disposal of Jews, Russian Communists, and other subhuman species. Purification by fire.

The Mercedes stopped directly in front of adjoined warehouses. The outside was grayish, concrete, stuccoed or wood. Anonymous. As a man who knew a thing or two about art and architecture, Hitler approved.

He was quickly ushered out of the car into the long, narrow building. There were numerous partitions and lighting was low intensity. A humming sound emanated from the rear.

A nervous man in a white lab coat appeared, accompanied by others behind him, dressed the same, thrusting their arms, and chorusing "*Heil Hitler.*"

"There are more faithful German technical experts busy in the work area," Horst Wessel said. "They work around the clock to bring this project to completion."

Impatiently, Hitler turned to Wessel, who understood the silent message and pointed at the greeters and shouted orders, demanding facts, demanding them now.

The man in the white lab coat was shoved forward, carrying a folder. He seemed to shrink inside his lab coat, a small man with tightly-curled hair, thick glasses, and a hooked nose. This Jew was exactly as Reinhard had described and Hitler had visualized: a mad scientist. Reinhard and his delightful sense of humor.

A subhuman, yes, but an idiot savant with a gift for beneficial science. Reinhard had assured Hitler that this Jew was as intelligent as the traitorous one who escaped Germany in 1933, Albert Einstein.

Let him live up to his madness. Or else!

Wessel smirked. "His name is—"

Normally apoplectic in the close proximity of a Jew, Hitler was remarkably composed. Truth be told, his apoplexy in the company of a Jew or a Communist was partly an act, justifying anything and everything he did to them.

Hitler lifted a finger, silencing the attaché. To him, Jews had no names; they had numbers tattooed on their arms. After this mad scientist was of no further benefit to the Reich, he would be reunited with his loved ones. Those of them that were still alive. The Aryan underlings here, regrettably, were destined for the same fate. They had eyes, mouths and voices.

The scientist's absurdly incongruous name, that so amused Horst Wessel, was Ira Pendleton-Hume. The outrageously British surname was the result of a drunken union in 1899 between a British cavalry officer during the Second Boer War and a half-Jewish housemaid, an embarrassment to Lieutenant Pendleton-Hume and a secret from the dashing officer's wife who awaited him at home, busying herself with teas and a dalliance of her own with a ministry undersecretary of nothing important. With a combination of threats and monetary encouragement, mother and son emigrated to Palestine.

A labyrinthine series of affairs and marriages and sibling births led them throughout the British Isles and mainland Europe. Ira was beyond bright, at age 22, a physics PhD at Oxford. Still a callow youth, he became the family patriarch, hanging on to a fellowship at the University of Vienna a tad too long.

In 1938, in the aftermath of the German *Anschluss*—or Nazi occupation—he and his extended family were scooped up by the conquerors. Ira was presented with a proposition he had no choice but to accept. He was to stand by for any assignment where his brilliance was requisite. The German researchers had learned their lesson with the absent Einstein. To remain available, the heavily-guarded Ira had been installed in a filthy Berlin crackerbox of an apartment until transferred to Lisbon.

In the Nazi's pseudo-science of eugenics and phrenology. it made no difference if you were half-Jewish or one-percent Jewish or, paraphrasing the American Ivory Snow soap advertisement, 99 44/100% pure Aryan. A Jew was a Jew was a Jew. The lives of Ira's aging mother, three children, aunts, uncles, cousins, and friends were totally dependent on his cooperation and performance. They had tattooed a number on Ira's arm, to make sure that he knew his place, to know that they had a spot reserved for him too if he faltered or resisted.

"What do you have for me," Hitler ordered. "I haven't got all night."

Roughly, Wessel tore the folder from the scientist's hands and opened it. "You have of course heard of the Radium Girls, *mein Führer*."

"Of course I have," Hitler lied. "So?"

"Yes, of course, absolutely, but if I may quickly summarize for my colleagues who are not as enlightened as you, fifteen to twenty-five years ago—the Radium Girls, as they were known—worked in the United States at watch factories painting radium on the numbers of watch faces so they could be seen in the dark. The girls were instructed to lick their tiny brushes to keep the points sharp, having been told as they worked that radium was harmless. Some even painted their nails with it."

The scientist paused, cleared his throat, removed photographs from the folder, and handed them to Hitler.

"This is proof that radium is not harmless."

Hitler sorted through pictures of young women with portions of their jaws missing and large skin blotches. One shot was of a naked woman on an autopsy slab, her face grotesque, her last vestiges of life in obvious agony. At the sight of her anguish rather than her pubic region, Hitler felt a stirring below his belt. He handed the photos back before he began noticeably perspiring.

Wessel said, "We arranged for a shipment of enriched uranium called yellowcake. It was mined and processed in Africa, in the Belgian Congo by their ape men and shipped to us in barges covered with ears of corn. The Congo has the world's richest uranium ore, or uraninite, as much as seventy-percent pure. This is processed into the yellowcake. While Belgium and thus their colonies has joined the Reich, the British and Americans are seeking this ore too, but we have access to an adequate supply of it."

Hitler said, his voice rising, "You are showing me radium sickness. Why are you speaking of this uranium substance?"

"These people work with uranium, *mein Führer*," Wessel said, pointing to the rear. "They have found a way to further enrich this uranium, an isotope many times more radioactive than the Radium Girls' radium. This is the isotope that someday will be the core of a massive bomb."

Hitler had heard wild talk of such a bomb, but dismissed it as a secret weapon of the distant future. He cared about weapons *now*.

He smiled coldly. "A bomb?"

"So powerful that if dropped on London, the city will become a crater, as lifeless as one on the moon."

"Your talk of bombs. You say they are in the future. Has there been progress here? When can you have this bomb for me? I do not tolerate doubletalk!"

Wessel flinched. The *Führer* could be childlike in his shifting attention and his demands. Is he the most complex man who ever lived?

He said, "I'm sorry to say that a bomb is many years in the future if at all, and it is beyond the capabilities of this facility to accomplish. What we have made is too impure to even think of a bomb at this time."

"Then why have you wasted my time bringing me here?" Hitler screamed, snapping his fingers as he often did on the ragged edge of one of his frightening rages that could last for hours. "Are you teasing me with promises you cannot fulfill?"

A quavering Horst Wessel said, "*mein Führer*, we are at the brink of manufacturing something superior and in required quantities, within weeks if not days, which will cause acute radiation poisoning to our enemies."

As if a switch had been tripped, Hitler calmed down and looked at the Jew scientist in what passed for him as serenity.

Ira Pendleton-Hume, said, "Sir, that background humming sound we hear is a cyclotron, which is a particle accelerator. The cyclotron I have devised can extract the most radioactive of uranium isotopes. It is the smallest cyclotron ever made and can operate in secrecy, requiring substantially less power than others in development elsewhere."

"Yes, this is true. Nevertheless, the machine requires much electricity for buildings such as this that appear from the outside to be of no use," Horst Wessel said, rubbing thumb and forefinger together. "But I have worked this out with Lisbon's public works administrators."

Hitler ignored the self-serving comments and said, "What value is this uranium isotope, as you call it, to the Reich? The value *now*?"

Horst Wessel, Lisbon's chief SS attaché, wasn't a scientist. He didn't know and was afraid to say he didn't. Nervously, he took a cigarette from his pocket and a lighter with a swastika on it, and produced a flame.

Hitler turned to him. Thinking better of smoking, Wessel dropped the cigarette and crushed it with a toe. The *Führer* did not smoke, drank little, and was a vegetarian. He was a very strange man in many respects.

The impatient *Führer* looked at the scientist, who forced a yellow-toothed smile and flattened his hands. "We can pulverize the powder so it can be dropped from an airplane over a city."

"It isn't a gas?"

Wessel said, "No, *mein Führer*. It will be a powder finer than cake flour, yet it won't drift. Uranium is among the heaviest of elements. The powder will drop straight down, where it has been aimed."

"Heaviest of elements? Heavier than lead?"

Ignoramus, Ira Pendleton-Hume thought. Adolf Hitler was a vicious beast whose knowledge of the planet was confined to methods of destroying life on it. Uranium was close to twice as heavy as lead.

Ira said, "Heavier than even tungsten and gold and most elements on the periodic table. It will fall—plunging, if you will—unnoticed on London, if as I have been informed, it is a much desired target, and then properly dissipate and cling unnoticed to whatever it falls upon."

Horst Wessel said, "If I may suggest, as a diversion, combine the drop with the release of Dr. Goebbels's wonderful informational leaflets."

Hitler liked that idea. Joseph Goebbels was as loyal and obedient as a lap dog. Goebbels had words for any occasion. It was he who said that if you repeat a lie long enough, it will be accepted as the truth.

"Go on."

Horst Wessel said, "The London enemies will walk in the powder, tracking it home. They will breathe it. If they stupidly wad up and discard Dr. Goebbels' illuminating messages, the deadly powder will be on their hands. As he said, it is impure, diluted, so it will react with soft tissue gradually, extending the period of discomfort."

"And?"

Horst Wessel jabbed a finger at the folder.

Ira Pendleton-Hume withdrew more photos for Hitler, eight-by-ten glossies of dead men who appeared to be 100 years old, as if wretches who had succumbed to smallpox.

Barely able to get the hateful description out, he said, "Initially, there will be nausea and vomiting. Then nosebleeds and sores in many cases. Radiation inhibits the body's ability to regenerate red blood cells. Aplastic anemia and bone marrow degeneration. Neurological damage too. Death does not always come rapidly. These men suffered enormously."

"Who are they?"

"Alas," Wessel said. "Careless German technicians."

Hitler glared at him.

"But most are busybody locals who strayed by. Homeless refugees nobody will miss."

"How rapidly will death come?"

Ira Pendleton-Hume said, "It is not possible to say because of variables. The amount absorbed, the body's resistance— "

"Will there be discomfort in each and every case such as these in the photographs?"

Horst Wessel beamed. "Yes, *mein Führer*. It will be hideously unpleasant."

Hitler nodded approvingly. "Your powder can be made to fall on Buckingham Palace and 10 Downing Street too?"

"Yes, yes. Because of its weight, release of the powder can be precise, regardless of wind and other conditions."

"England," Hitler said dreamily, thinking *Winston Churchill*. "There are eight million people in London."

"With enough powder, we can kill one million of them."

"Only one million?" Hitler said.

Wessel spread his hands. "Well, two million. Three. Who can say until it's done? The purity and volume of the powder are unknowns."

Hitler nodded again, digesting this.

Wessel said, "A long-range aircraft could reach America too, should they be so foolish as to enter the war against us. New York, Washington, D.C. We have aircraft now that can make the flight one-way. It would be a suicide mission, of course, because the plane could not carry sufficient gasoline to return home. I know there would be a multitude of volunteers willing to sacrifice their lives for such a great cause, knowing they would be honored even beyond the thousand years of the Third Reich.

"I have done research, *Mein Fuhrer*. Lisbon is Europe's most westerly city. It will be child's play to fly an airplane from here to the United States. Should you so desire."

Hitler studied the faces of the Radium Girls, his favorite picture.

"I will take these photographs with me. To compare them to the result you have guaranteed me. When will you have enough of this poisonous uranium? This processed poison."

"Weeks at the most," Ira said, tensely, as if expecting a swat. He bore a strong resemblance to the Jewish men depicted in the Nazis' vile propaganda posters, an appearance that in the past had troubled him. Not now. He was proud to resemble the antithesis of the Aryan ideal.

Hitler said, "I will continue to give you what you need. The amount of funding and its source will be unchanged, as will modifications to the airplane slated to drop this deadly uranium powder of yours. There will be no excuses tolerated for delay and this insistence on gold, not Reichsmarks or Portuguese escudos troubles me."

"I assure you, *mein Führer*," Wessel said. "Nobody will be the wiser as to how the money flows, no matter how much. Paper money is suspect in these unsettled times, even Reichsmarks and Swiss francs. Gold has been magical throughout history. Gold and the promise of more gold buys productivity and silence."

Hitler thought for a few seconds, then said, "If gold is required beyond what I authorize today, the responsibility is yours. The Reich requires gold for expenses to maintain soldiers on the ground, airmen and submariners. Your experimental radiation poison is appealing, but experimental it is. Do you understand?"

Horst Wessel anticipated this. Expenses beyond the initial estimate too. There were methods for mining gold other than digging in the ground for it, and he had one method in mind. Portuguese intelligence sources were spotty, he knew, but they did occasionally yield a gem.

He clicked his heels together. "Yes, of course, *mein Führer*."

Hitler ended the meeting without comment by turning around and marching out.

In the car on the way to the airport, Wessel saw from the corner of an eye that Hitler was holding the pictures tightly with perspiring hands. Intuitively, he knew that he should not speak unless his *Führer* spoke first.

Horst Wessel had always desperately wanted to please anyone and everyone, for as long as he could remember, most often unsuccessfully. He had wanted to be somebody for as long as he could remember.

One of three children of a bookkeeper and a housewife in Bremen, a family of no consequence, he was small for his age and somewhat withdrawn. He had been brutalized by other kids in the Hitler Youth. Wessel had a growth spurt late in adolescence, reaching average height. Thanks to a physical fitness regimen, he was no longer one to be trifled with.

In addition, through the immortal Horst Wessel—a name change he had made two years ago—Wessel had succeeded beyond any expectation; he was *somebody*. As a doppelgänger of his own making and his role in the radioactive uranium, he would appear in history books throughout the 1000-year Reich, a man who had aided his *Führer* in destroying his most-hated enemy.

*****

On the ride to the airport, and later on the malodorous flight to Berlin, Adolf Hitler fidgeted, but didn't utter a word.

HISTORICAL NOTE: Neither Adolf Hitler, nor Reinhard Heydrich, one of his favorite fiends-in-waiting, ever visited Lisbon. They may have or may not have done some of the other things that follow.

CHAPTER 2

July 4, 1940. Independence Day far, far away.

In Lisbon, just another Thursday.

At dusk, a cloudless 85 degrees, Horatio Alger (Harry) Antonelli mopes through Lisbon's Alfama district, achingly homesick on this special day. At Christmas and New Year's Eve, you can always find somebody of any nationality and political slant to hoist a few with. But today, even if he had firecrackers, not even Harry Antonelli is reckless enough to light them off. Lisbon is hair-trigger, incendiary.

Harry's dogs are barking.

Lisbon's seven hills mean business. Much of Lisbon is old, but not ancient. On All Saints Day, November 1, 1755, earthquakes rattling dishware as far as Glasgow flattened it. Candles burning in churches set fires that burned whatever hadn't been shaken into rubble. An Atlantic tsunami rolled up the Rio Tejo, finishing the job. Lisbon has been virtually rebuilt.

Up Harry goes on a tendon-stretching switchback, past the *Sé*, the city's twin-towered cathedral, headed toward *Castelo de São Jorge* (Castle of Saint George) that sits atop the hill, it and its 16th-century cannons keeping watch over Lisbon.

He takes a gander down at orange trees heavy with ripe fruit. Lisbon's red-tile roofs and whitewashed walls fade to the hazy fringes of town.

The 1755 temblor did spare large parts of the Alfama. It is a maze, hilly and unruly. In five minutes, a stranger will become hopelessly lost.

The Alfama was here when the Visigoths were. Some narrow streets haven't seen direct sun in centuries, some so narrow that Harry can touch buildings on both sides at once.

He is a block from his flat. Fortunately, he doesn't see his landlady, an old chain-smoking, red-nosed sourpuss, but nevertheless crosses the street in a hurry. If she nabs him for back rent, she'll announce an increase on the spot, payable in advance.

Refugees from the Low Countries via France and via Spain are gobbling up every square foot of accommodations. Owners are renting by the week and day, packing them in spare rooms, double-bunked as if in military barracks, so she'll be happy for an excuse to toss Harry out on his ear.

Meanwhile, government big shots are putting on an expensive shindig, The Portuguese World Exhibition of 1940, the *Esposição do Mundo Português*, in Belém, along the river just west of Lisbon. Harry sees it as a kid brother to New York's World's Fair of last year. With gingerbread buildings and exhibits, it celebrates the founding of the nation in 1140 and restoration of independence from Spain in 1640. It's costing a fortune Portugal doesn't have. But when you're ruled by a dictator, you do what he wants you to do, and this is his baby.

To complicate things, the Duke of Windsor and that American gal he gave up the throne to marry arrived yesterday, passing through, headed to who knows where. Trailing behind them is more luggage than you could fit in five Greyhound buses. Cars, too, in their caravan, and their maid.

The Duchess is no kid, but she's still a tomato who's gone through two husbands and knows the score. Harry wouldn't mind having her on his arm for a date or two, and whatever that leads to. She's skinny for his taste, but he wouldn't kick her out of bed, though dropping to a knee, offering her a diamond, he can't picture himself doing that.

All those Brit royals have been inbred for generations and that guy, the Duke, is said not to be too bright. They also say that the Germans have him twisted around their little finger.

On the other hand, Harry supposes that having some fun with the Duchess is preferable to sitting around in a palace with a crown on your head and nothing to do except twiddle your thumbs and knight people, putting your sword on their shoulders. Something Harry would charge them to do.

Anyway, it's Churchill who really runs the country and the war.

They aren't the only swells beelining it through Lisbon. Among them is Peggy Guggenheim, a rich New York society dame, who collects art and artists, along with her latest, a surrealist by the name of Max Ernst. Harry has seen some of Ernst's stuff. Him and other surrealists, they paint reality as it looks after too long at a bar drinking cheap hootch. Harry knows this by experience.

Another pair to draw to is King Carol II of Romania and his gal, Madame Lupescu, who spend most of their time in the Estoril casino out by the coast. He's seen pictures of them. The king is Jack Spratt and his wife "could eat no lean".

All of Europe now is crazy, nuts. Harry Antonelli had graduated from the University of Washington with a degree in history, quite aware that he was and is in the midst of it being made. That awareness is becoming less and less comfortable.

Harry goes to a newsstand. German papers and propaganda magazines are clothes-pinned to racks. Anywhere you go, you can't avoid Hitler and his slobbering goons.

He picks up a July 1 *New York Times* from a thin pile in front of the cash register. It's the most recent edition they have. Harry always starts at the sports section. It's like eating your dessert first.

As usual, soccer is all over the sports pages, an oddball sport they call football or *fútbol*. You can't use your hands, for Chrissake. Not like the real football he'd played where you use your hands and forehead and shoulders and everything else you can get away with. In this soccer of theirs, you kick the ball all over the field for 90 minutes, and if it ends 0-0, that's how they leave it, and nobody minds. Very strange.

There's a small corner box of baseball scores. His hometown Pacific Coast League Seattle Rainiers had knocked off the Hollywood Stars, 6-2. Good for them. Looks like they're on their way to winning another pennant.

They have an important series coming up with the San Francisco Seals. Thank goodness, the Yankees had signed Joe DiMaggio, but the Seals still have guys who can knock the hide off the ball.

Harry had a baseball bat in his hands for as long as he could remember. He'd played baseball in high school. Swinging for the outfield seats, he could hit it a mile, tying the school record for home runs in his senior year, but for the life of him couldn't hit a good curveball or field a hot grounder. He was all power, no refinement. The story of his life.

HISTORICAL NOTE: The three preceding paragraphs dubiously speculate that The New York Times has any interest whatsoever in Pacific Coast League baseball.

There are no comics in this newspaper, a serious shortcoming. Harry likes the daily funny papers and *loves* the Sunday funnies, a separate section in color. He loves them more than ever as there is nothing funny about Europe these days.

Hungry for English-language news of any sort, he reads a front-page story, ignoring the glaring newsstand owner, who knows Harry by sight and knows that he isn't going to buy.

SEVERE PENALTIES FACED BY FRENCH. *German Army Decrees Death for Those Retaining Arms and Radio Senders. GUERRILLAS WILL BE SHOT. Reich Laws Applicable to All Cases Brought Before Military for Trial.*

Tacked on is a long list of infractions. No radios or anti-Nazi pamphlets or unauthorized meetings. No firearms permitted. Blow your nose without written permission from the Gestapo and you'll be bumped off by a firing squad without a trial beforehand. They're judge and jury while they're setting you up in front of sandbags, the dirty Kraut bastards.

He looks at another paper without touching it, thinking the propaganda rag has germs. *Kill a German in an occupied country and 100 locals will be shot.* Nice.

Sadistic sons of bitches, Harry thinks, replacing the paper, smiling at the unsmiling vendor. Do things the Nazi way or say your prayers. Harry knows firsthand what the swastika boys are like. And secondhand, Germans in general.

His uncle Fred had served in the Great War, the 1914 War, the War to End All Wars. Uncle Fred had flown a Sopwith Camel. He'd been shot down by a German, a member of their Flying Circus. Some claimed by Manfred von Richthofen in his Fokker tri-wing, the Red Baron himself. Others said Hermann Göring pulled the trigger. Göring was a crack aviator then before he joined up with Hitler and his gangsters, and packed on 300 pounds of lard.

Portugal straddles the political fence. Like in football, if your opponent is faster and stronger, you're gonna get the living daylights beaten out of you. The Portuguese sure as hell know that.

Harry heads downhill on the next street, but because of the heat and uneven pavement, it isn't much easier than uphill. Around a cobblestoned corner is Maria Fernanda Ramos's 1935 Citroën, half up on the sidewalk, a jalopy the size of a desk with scabrous black paint. Once upon a time, its bug-eye chrome headlamps had been shiny silver, but now they are pitted, like they have the measles.

TECHNICAL NOTE: It is a 1935 Citroen Twelve Saloon with suicide doors, a 9' 6½" wheelbase, and 12.8 horsepower engine. Despite advanced features like hydraulic brakes, "Monoshell" body, and front-wheel drive, Harry's cynical description is probably correct.

Her car is jam-packed with cinched cloth bags.

In the bags, Harry knows: counterfeit wine corks, stamped with vintages they will never plug.

Maria Fernanda is getting a cut on the deal for providing the transportation, negotiated by the man Harry is meeting in the bar.

There are 75 sorely-needed escudos in the deal for him once their boy at the port takes delivery. Twenty-five escudos worth of back rent and grub on the table. Or he can spend it on something useful. As tired as he is of being a nickels-and-dimes guy, Harry will sigh in relief for every coin in his hands.

He walks into the Café do Canção (Café of Song) , a popular *fado* bar, a squarish room twice the size of a high school classroom. It's as dark as a closet, with a bar, a small stage, and a useless ceiling fan that paddles slabs of warm air.

The walls are decorated with tobacco-tar-stained posters of Portuguese sights: the Algarve beaches in August and its sunbathers covering most of the sand, Estoril resort hotels beyond the reach of most of the Canção patrons, impoverished, picturesque hill towns, and the rough Atlantic coastline.

And of course, a poster of Prime Minister António de Oliveira Salazar, Portugal's dictator, standing at a balcony keeping watch over this bar and everything else inside Portugal's borders. Handsome and statesmanlike, looking deceptively like an ordinary businessman in suit and tie, the Prime Minister is watching closely.

Harry focuses through the smoke at the usual clientele: *Lisboetas,* Brits, Germans, Spaniards, Italians. Some he knows, most he doesn't. Half are spies and/or smugglers who trade lies and rumors in six languages. No cooler inside than out, more patrons than not wear jackets, not to be formal but to conceal whatever it is they're concealing.

Harry Antonelli feels right at home in the Canção.

Peter Owen jabs a finger at Hitler's neck as Harry sits down with him.

Harry signals for a glass of *vinho tinto*, green or young wine, his usual here. You can't get a decent glass of beer in Lisbon and local cigarettes smell like a car fire. Thanks to the war, American cigarettes are on the black market, but costing a small fortune.

It's enough to make you quit smoking and drinking, Harry thinks, sipping his wine and lighting a Camel.

"What're you in an uproar about now, Peter?"

"Feast your eyes at him, Harry."

Harry looks at Peter's newspaper and a photo of a sour, bug-eyed little man with a stupid mustache, walking on the *Champs-Élysées* with a mob of Nazi big shots—boot lickers wearing jackboots. In case anybody's curious what his latest conquest is, the *Arc de Triomphe* is in the background.

Peter Owen is perhaps five years older than Harry's 24, perhaps 10 years. He's short and ruddy, and claims to be a Brit. Mostly he does sound British, but sometimes not, lapsing in and out of a bad Noel Coward. Accents and slang roll in and out of all sides of his mouth, Dutch and Spanish and Portuguese, now and then a brief slippage into middle America. And some dialects so unrecognizable that they could be from the planet Mongo, home of Ming the Merciless.

Whenever Harry presses Peter on his shifting speech patterns, he shifts to a cockney that requires an interpreter.

"So?" Harry says.

Peter's voice rises, as it does after too many Scotches or glasses of port. When he's "pissed" as the Brits put it.

"So? Sew buttons on your bloody shoes. See him, king of the Boche, smug and sidelong here with his mates? Hitler doesn't drink and he's a vegetarian. The only vegetarians in the world are mental patients and East Indians I knew when I served on the Subcontinent with the raj. They were starving to death while cattle roamed the streets of Bombay. The wogs wouldn't touch them."

"Wherever you're going with this, your Nazis and East Indians and vegetarians, you don't have to do a sales job on me, Peter, selling I don't know what. From what I've seen of Europe, the Earth is flat and Hitler has a barbed-wire fence around it."

"Barbed wire. Jolly good, Harry. Where was I? Yes. The Nazis are locusts, you know, mechanized locusts. Mark my words. They'll be goose-stepping in Madrid and Lisbon within a month or two. Salazar's as neutral as Franco. Switzerland neutral too? Ha! They're Hitler's fences, his financial whores. A pawn shop of a nation it is, trying to gather up more gold than Midas. Yours, mine, anybody's gold. I'd bet my last shilling that Swiss bankers have swastikas tattooed on their bums and their willies, every bloody one of the blighters."

"Peter—"

"Listen to me, Harry. It's so bloody simple. Wolfram, Portugal's tungsten ore, which they have gobs of, is shipped to Germany on the sly, so England doesn't find out and get in a big snit. Germany ships gold to Swiss banks. Swiss francs go into Portugal's account. Portugal buys gold with the Swiss francs. A bloody fine golden triangle."

"Your gold? My gold? What brought this on out of nowhere?"

Peter nods at his glass of Scotch, his usual answer when he doesn't have one.

Harry says, "The last gold I saw was a Stanford quarterback's tooth I knocked out. Lisping, he called me something that concerned my mother. The ref heard, translated, and gave them fifteen yards."

"You and what you over in the Colonies call football, the football that you played, dressed up like soldiers, beating each other's brains out? I did not understand a word you said."

Harry doubts that, but lets it pass. "Gold, Peter. Gold."

"A figure of speech, Harry."

Harry shakes his head.

Peter changes the subject by looking at the wall poster and muttering, "Bloody Salazar."

Harry doesn't think Prime Minister António de Oliveira Salazar is an angel. He may be a fascist in sheep's clothing, but at least he doesn't stuff himself into a uniform like a sausage and strut as Hitler,

Mussolini and Franco do, or call himself *caudillo* or *duce* or *führer*, all meaning "boss". He lives like a monk, working 25 hours a day, dedicated to his country, so he's not the worst despot who ever lived.

Salazar reads the direction of the wind and who can blame him? Peter's right. If Spain joins the Axis side, Portugal is doomed, squashed by Spanish and German troops inside of a week. What Harry had seen in Madrid, fascists shooting people at random and knocking heads, he wouldn't be surprised by anything. He's seen no book burnings in Lisbon as he had in Germany and Austria, though, a saving grace.

Finger to his lips, Harry says, "Pipe down."

"*Der Führer's* trousers are around his ankles and Salazar's on his knees. His bosom chum, Hitler, he can take this country whenever he wants simply by picking up the phone."

"Pipe down," Harry repeats, looking around. "You're not in London, you know. The definition of treason is different here and you just committed it."

"Yes, London. My countrymen are no better. For God's sake, the Anglo-Portuguese treaty was signed in 1373, the oldest agreement in Europe. Even if it was scribbled on parchment, what should be the difference?"

"Peter, stop your goddamn yelling," Harry yells. "Save your damn history lessons too. I majored in history, remember?"

"Don't get me started on the Bolsheviks, Harry. Communists and their utopia."

Harry raises his right hand. "I promise I won't."

As Peter resumes a staring contest with his Scotch, Harry wonders what's gotten into him. Their politics are the same, charter membership in the Me, Myself and I Party. Maybe he's jealous of Adolf Hitler. Harry and Peter live day-to-day by their wits, often on the fringes of the law, while Boss Adolf turned an entire nation into a criminal gang. Compared to Hitler, Al Capone and Lucky Luciano are small potatoes.

Harry knows Hitler's Germany all too well. While bumming around Europe after college graduation, he had been at the wrong place at the wrong time: Berlin, November 9, 1938, the first of two days of *Kristallnacht*. Meaning Crystal Night or the Night of Broken Glass. A scene out of Dante's Inferno. A nation of juvenile delinquents, including the police, who instead of guarding and protecting, joined in the fun.

Had he been able to understand German, he would have known that in Paris, on November 7th, a 17-year-old Polish Jew had shot to death a German diplomat. This was regarded as an organized political assassination, a Hebrew conspiracy, a pretext for a *Kristallnacht* rampage that burned 267 synagogues, vandalized 7500 Jewish businesses, killed as many as 100 Jews, and rounded up 30,000 Jewish males for shipment to concentration camps.

Regardless, as a history major, Harry should have known better and scrammed right out of town the day he arrived, a week earlier. He couldn't remember any tyrant coaxing his subjects to behave so badly, like rabid animals. Genghis Khan, Caligula, Ivan the Terrible, none of them. Hitler was one of a fucking kind.

Frenzied mobs were breaking faces as well as windows. You couldn't walk down the street without crunching on glass or tripping over a human being, either unconscious or worse. Harry was all set to hustle into an alley for the night, sleep in a doorway to save money, and hop the first train out of town in the morning.

Before he could, he was set upon by a pack of thugs who decided that an American of Scottish-Italian persuasion whose nose had been broken playing college football appeared Jewish. They had demanded that he thrust the Nazi salute. Not one to ever exercise common sense and back down, Harry obliged, modifying it with a middle finger. Thinking as they came at him that he sure could use Buck Rogers' ray gun.

In preparation for such an occasion in Europe's growingly-uncomfortable environment, Harry had been uncharacteristically moderate in food and drink, to keep football muscle from turning into beer fat. Him being a cigarette smoker was also an advantage to his physique. He knew of doctors who advised their patients to take up the habit to lose weight. Got a spare tire? Like the slogan says, *Reach for a Lucky instead of a Sweet,* although he wouldn't Walk a Mile for a Camel, his favorite brand.

When they tore into him, Harry created enough emergency dental work to keep a clinic happy. The leader, a soft-looking fella with a weak chin, came at him first with a lead pipe.

Harry had been a placekicker as well as a halfback for the University of Washington Huskies. Imagining a 30-yarder straight through the uprights, he made the lead-pipe wielder eligible for the Vienna Boys Choir with his 10-DDD, an act that unfortunately would follow him.

They prevailed in numbers. Next morning, Harry looked like he'd bobbed for apples in a hornet's nest. Having worn out his welcome in a country the Nazis had turned into an insane asylum, he used documents he'd stolen from one of his attackers in the melee and crossed into Austria, six months after the *Anschluss* or German annexation, jumping from the fire into the frying pan.

Horatio Alger (Harry Antonelli) is no friend of the Nazis, but in the here and now, he has learned that it's smart to keep your politics to yourself and your trap shut.

At long last, Peter does pipe down, drinking his Scotch.

"Is João coughing up our dough?" Harry says.

He has never liked or trusted João, a short, thin, weaselly guy with wispy hair who never looks you in the eye. Peter is evasive how he connected with João, as he is on many subjects. Harry knows better than to be mixed up with Peter in general, just as he knows better than to do a multitude of other things he does.

"If the bloke wants the corks, he will."

"So where is he, this bloody bloke of yours?"

Peter waves his empty glass at the bartender like a semaphore.

"They're going to be shipped momentarily. He's acquiring slate for ballast. It has to be of the proper size and weight to match the olive oil stamps on the crates. Corks are lightweight, you realize. Once we establish a cork connection generally, we'll look in other markets. Cork goes into gaskets and washers for aeroplanes so fluids don't seep and leak."

"Thanks for the mechanical science lesson. If he doesn't find slate, then what? Maria Fernanda's car is outside, stuffed to the gills."

"Harry, don't worry. You'll worry yourself into an ulcer. Have I ever told you that you Yanks are bloody pushy?"

"Not in the last two days."

"How long have you been in Lisbon, mate?"

"You know how long. Too long," Harry says. "Coming on eight months. After I wore out my welcome in Madrid, Vienna and Brussels and Amsterdam. And Budapest."

"End of the line, eh?"

"I think so. I'm getting homesick."

Harry neglects to add that when he arrives home in Seattle, whenever that might be, he will be expected to have grown up. And expected to behave responsibly and maturely. A host of unfair demands.

"You've gone native, that's what you've done here, Harry. *Engage*, the French call it when their Legionnaires posted in French Indochina can't resist the inscrutable Orient and their exotic slant-eyed ladies. Lisbon is every bit as inscrutable as Saigon or Hanoi, wouldn't you say? In this town, you are wise to expect the unexpected."

Harry drinks his wine and smokes, looking at nothing, relegating Peter to background noise, ignoring any further enlightenment.

Maria Fernanda Ramos comes from backstage to applause, Harry's is the loudest as he jumps to his feet. The Canção's lead *fado* singer, Maria Fernanda is dark and sultry in flowered skirt and silken blouse, doe-eyed, a hint of Moorish in her lovely face. She bears a resemblance to an actress he really likes: Lupe Vélez, the Mexican Spitfire.

Fado means fate in Portuguese. *Fado's* mournful lyrics speak of the vagaries of fate and how you usually wind up getting it in the neck. Resignation and melancholia, all that. To Harry, the tunes are nearly as lovely as Maria Fernanda.

Maria Fernanda blows him a kiss and begins to sing, accompanied by an old-timer on a 12-string *guitarra*. Harry melts into a puddle of syrup, the only foreign regular in the Canção who gets weepy and he doesn't understand a single word of the lyrics.

Peter nudges him. "Pull yourself together, Harry. How many times do I have to tell you? Men don't cry in public, for God's sake. They do not. People will think you're a pooftah, a ponce. This is the last drinking establishment in the world for that. You'll end up in the gutter, flat on your back with a lump on the bean. Me too, guilty by association."

Harry replies by blowing his nose and wiping his eyes.

Just as Maria Fernanda finishes *Amar* (Love), which Harry *knows* is meant for him and only him, two beady-eyed fat necks swagger in, a pair of baby grands. They wear dark suits and bowler hats.

Bar atmosphere goes from dreamy to butt-puckering.

They might as well be wearing big red nametags, Harry thinks: PVDE.

Harry is reminded yet again that he should harbor no illusions about neutral Lisbon. Prime Minister Salazar's Portugal is a police state and police states have secret police, a fact of life Harry knows by experience. The PVDE or *Policia de Vigilância e de Estado* (Police of Vigilance and State Defense) is headquartered here in the capital, in a blockhouse of a building atop a hill in the Chiado district. It has a grand view of the city and the river from the outside, maybe not so swell a view from inside.

The PVDE is highly skilled at torture, having apprenticed to the Gestapo. Techniques range from the medieval thumbscrew to "standing torture", when prisoners are made to stand in tiny cells for days at a time. There are any number of stories in this City of Wild Tales and Rumors, so many that the odds are that they're true.

The two agents are immediately served by a nervous waiter, who brings a dusty bottle of port that is as old as Harry. There's no scratch on the table and Harry doesn't expect to see any.

"Is our penny-ante deal why these mugs are here, Peter?"

"I don't like coincidences."

"Is that yes or no?"

"Best you go check on the lass's motorcar," Peter says, eyes locked on his Scotch. "Be casual in the event they have a mate on the sidewalk keeping an eye out."

"Always me doing our dirty work," Harry complains, getting up.

He makes a self-consciously casual trip to the restroom, then slips out the back door and around the side of the building. Passersby stare at the overly nonchalant foreigner.

As he fears, Maria Fernanda's flivver is gone. Harry walks around the block and the next block, looking for it. No luck.

Back into the Canção. To an empty table. Peter is gone and the PVDE goons are gone.

Harry sits, trying hard to be calm, cool and collected. He takes deep breaths like coaches had told him to do after being carried off the field and given smelling salts.

Maria Fernanda completes her next selection that Harry barely hears, then sits with him.

"What's going on? Where's Peter?"

"Oh, Harry, the PVDE must have taken Peter away."

"You didn't see them?"

"I cannot look at those monsters. They have methods of knowing what is inside a person's soul."

"They're tidy. I'll say that for them. They cleaned off the table and stole my cigarettes too."

Maria Fernanda doesn't reply. She has made a habit of clamming up when things are uncomfortable, too often to suit Harry.

He gives her the bad news that her car is gone, corks and all.

Maria Fernanda looks at this American she wishes she could love unconditionally. But it will have to wait. Unconditional love comes with the same degree of trust; it could cost Maria Fernanda her life. At least this is what the romantic in Harry reads in her face.

Maria Fernanda pecks Harry's cheek and gets up for her next number. Leaning over, she whispers, "Oh well, the car was old and petrol is becoming so expensive. We will make new arrangements for corks. Go home and get some sleep. You look exhausted."

Meaning *go home alone*.

While she sings, Harry orders another *vinho tinto*, thinking that this latest scheme had been pillow talk, Maria Fernanda wearing nothing but perfume and a gauzy veil, putting on the latter after they'd made a mess of his bedding. He thinks of the veil as a metaphor for him and her, the distance she keeps even when they're intimate.

They always rendezvous at his dump. He doesn't know where she lives, doesn't know what she does when not in his bed or at the Canção. He doesn't know her past, her family members, even her age. Doesn't know from nothing, and when he presses for even the simplest answers, she tightens, almost physically shrinking. He's afraid if he pushes too hard, doesn't let up, regardless how eager he is for an answer, she'll fade away, as if a figment, a chimera.

"Harry," she had said. "The Nazis are turning Europe into a German sandbox. We all know this. It is hopeless to resist. Portugal can fall at any moment.

"Where will quality wine produced anywhere else come from? The finest French vintages your Detroit czars of Cadillac and Packard serve at their lavish dinner parties? Americans have coarse palates. They know nothing of wine but the labels and corks and price tags to boast of.

"Bottles and passable vintages can be made anywhere, but only from here can come the verifying corks. Portugal produces half the world's cork, did you know? Much of the rest comes from Spain that is controlled by that ugly little man in the funny uniform. To your Detroit and Wall Street moneybags, the boast is more important than the taste."

She then rattled off Château Such and Such 1928 and Domaine So and So 1931, the profit their buyers in America could get by bottling swill found in cheap bars with their counterfeit verification. If and when Portugal becomes a German colony, purveyors can claim they hoarded cases of rare vintages before the fall.

Being schooled in bed by her was infinitely preferable to talking to Peter in a bar. If Peter had posed the scheme, Harry might have said no, but how he can refuse Maria Fernanda and her veil? Harry has fallen for Maria Fernanda like a ton of bricks.

That this was a business scheme in partnership with Peter too should have made him wary. It did, but he ignored warning signs as he so frequently does. A red light of any sort is so often a challenge to him rather than a caution.

He finishes his wine and has another, moping. He wishes himself a Happy Independence Day, does a bottoms up, pays, and makes his way home. He goes into the street behind his flat, which is slightly narrower than the street in front. There are no fire escapes in his part of Alfama, so Harry jumps up to catch the deck of a tiny balcony, does a chin-up, grabs some decorative wrought iron and works his way up onto it. Very quietly. He doubts if his neighbors will be understanding.

He repeats the precarious callisthenic to his balcony, on the third floor of four.

He had left the door open because of the heat. He parts the threadbare curtains before entering.

Nobody is there, *nothing* is there. His meager belongings are gone.

Shit. Son of a bitch. Petty thievery. You can't trust anyone these days, he thinks.

No, wait. His landlady. Has to be.

Sure. She likes her port even more than her cigarettes. After a few glasses, she becomes testy, nasty, and unreasonable about little things. Like overdue rent. And lady friends staying late and leaving early, as if it's any of her business.

Harry tiptoes inside, thinking the worst, that she's dumped his few worldly possessions into the hallway, taking what she wants, and putting a padlock on the hallway door.

But the door is cracked.

He creeps to it. Three long steps and he's there. His home-sweet-home is a single room with the bathroom at the end of the hall. He isn't living at the Ritz.

The hallway light is out; the old woman is as cheap about the building's electricity as everything else.

Harry squints out at a silhouette. Somebody's sitting on something next to a pile of something.

Slowly, he leans forward and sticks his head all the way out.

"Happy Fourth of July, Antonelli."

CHAPTER 3

Dazed, befuddled, and stupefied, Harry holds onto whatever he can for support, a rotted door-jamb that begins to crumble. He releases it and makes his way into the hallway.

"Dorothy?"

"You haven't forgotten my voice, Horatio? I'm surprised. It has been ages."

It is Dorothy. Dorothy Booth. When she had been out of sorts with him, he wasn't Harry, he was Antonelli or Horatio or, at the very worst, Horatio Alger.

Dorothy is sitting on Harry's suitcase that is balanced unsteadily on a pile of his clothing, clean and unwashed. As she stands, he offers a helping hand, which she declines, moving out of his reach. Ever the independent lady, whether pissed off at him or not.

"I haven't forgotten your voice. I haven't forgotten you. I'm shocked that you're here and it's been a long day."

"I'm sorry to make it longer," she says. "My deepest apologies."

"Sling all the arrows you want, Dorothy. I deserve it."

"I got here just as your landlady was dumping all of this out of your room. She was grumpy and smelled like a brewery."

"A port winery, actually."

"You really do live *here*?"

"I do."

Dorothy brushes by him, goes inside, flips on the light switch, and looks around. "Peeling paint, chunks of plaster missing. Walls and

34

ceiling the color of spoiled oatmeal. Cat-sized dust kittens."

"I haven't started my spring housekeeping yet," Harry says, too discombobulated to be offended.

"My conception of you as an adventurer, a soldier of fortune," she says, her voice trailing off into a sigh.

His 5'9" and 180 pounds shrinks to the size of a water boy.

"You're expecting Captain America?" he counters lamely. "Superman?"

"Still the cartoon worshipper."

"Worshipper. That's an exaggeration."

"I paid your back rent and the next week's too."

Stunned, Harry says, "Uh, thanks."

"Don't mention it. I guess you're wondering why I'm here," Dorothy says. "Why the generosity too."

Harry's eyes are adjusting to the dim light. Dorothy hasn't changed an iota. Green eyes and the smoothest complexion. Her permanent wave is right out of the beauty salon and inside her white blouse and dark pleated skirt that shows nary a wrinkle is the same classy chassis. A large purse matching her blouse is slung over a shoulder, a new style feature for her.

Two years ago, when Harry got off the rat-infested tramp steamer at Le Havre, he was already missing her. Knowing he had no intention of coming home after the summer, he felt like a dummy and a coward. Looking at her now, smelling her, close enough to touch her, he firmly believes that he ought to be in a straitjacket.

"Wondering is putting it mildly."

"This is the address on your last postcard home to your parents. Sent months ago. Literally ages ago."

Not a comfortable subject. One to be ignored if at all possible.

"Did you just get in?" he says.

"Okeydoke, we'll change the subject. After three long days with stops at stepping-stone islands, just this afternoon."

"You must've taken the Pan Am Clipper."

"We did. No U-boat torpedoes for this girl."

Harry is in equal parts curious and envious. The Clipper is a Boeing 314, a gigantic four-engine flying boat that carries as many as 36 passengers in total luxury.

The Clipper has two carpeted decks, one exclusively for the crew. The passenger deck sports a dining room, bar, and dressing rooms with hot and cold running water.. The plush seats convert into beds, and the five- and six-course meals are whipped up by chefs from four-star hotels, served by white-jacketed stewards. The silverware is real silver Harry could see himself pocketing.

With an intermediate stop in the Azores, it can make the New York to Lisbon flight in an unbelievable 20 hours. The only thing that slows it up is high waves in the Azores. If they're over 30 inches, they have to stand by for calmer seas before taking off.

Only the wealthiest refugees can afford to fly out of Lisbon in it. A one-way ticket costs $375 and $650 for a round-trip. From Harry's standpoint, it might as well be a million. Dorothy's dad is a dentist. Her mom's a housewife and she has an older brother too, so money isn't coming out of Dr. Booth's ears.

Harry is suspicious and then some. Who is the other part of *we*? Dorothy's here on her honeymoon, dropping by for *Auld Lang Syne*, rubbing his nose in it? But there's nothing on her ring finger, which Harry automatically checks on any gal. Lisbon's no honeymoon hot spot either. So what gives?

"We?"

"Never mind the fine details. I'm too tired to talk much longer."

Harry says, "Okay. We haven't gotten to the why."

"That too. We will later."

"Are you hungry or thirsty? Can I take you somewhere?"

"No thank you. Speaking of taking one somewhere, you took off after college graduation in '38 to spend the summer bumming around Europe, then teach at a high school and coach the football team. That was the last time I saw you."

"I thought you were too tired to talk much longer."

Dorothy looks at him.

All business, every question or comment is interrogation, an accusation, or a flat-out punch in the jaw. Harry knows he deserves it, but his mouth is parched from the heat and all the wine, and a headache is coming on, full blast.

"Honest, Dorothy, that was the basic plan. Everyone's expectation. After I was completely done with football, that is. The Chicago Cardinals called, you know. They offered me a train ticket and fifty bucks to come for a tryout as a defensive back. I played offense and defense in college, but I preferred defensive back, where I get to hit people rather than being hit."

"I remember. Everyone was so proud of you, but you are avoiding the main subject."

"Okay. As you know also, I passed on the pros. I made more in college after a good game than I would in the National Football League, when an alum slipped a few bucks in my hand. I'd seen the newsreels too. Those pros are giants. Across the line from them, they'd look like King Kong. Some weigh as much as two-twenty-five, two-thirty. There isn't enough leather and padding in the helmets. I'd be seeing stars on every play. They'd make mincemeat out of me."

"It was an honor they wanted to give you an audition, but you were wise not to. I was relieved. At the time," Dorothy says. "You don't have to make excuses. It would, however, be swell if you stay on the subject."

Harry gives up. "No pro football, so it was back to the basic plan. After the European summer, I'd teach history and coach high-school football. Settling down until I retire."

Not adding that it'd feel like a prison sentence. And that he is learning skills here not taught back home.

"It's been a long, long summer you spent bumming around Europe."

Harry feels her knife twisting. "There was always one more thing to see, and with Hitler gobbling up countries, I didn't think there'd ever be another chance. Now or never, you know."

Dorothy Booth's arms are folded. They had known each other since childhood. She first took notice of Harry at school recess. He liked to pick out the worst bullies on the playground and fight them, winning two-thirds of the time.

Why did he? Not to be a hero, a Robin Hood, he'd said, but to prove that he could. The bullied kids fell in love with him and so did pigtailed, prepubescent Dorothy Ann Booth.

When he did reach puberty, his physical maturity soared and his emotional maturity regressed. She couldn't keep track of all the windmills Harry tilted. In high school, Dorothy made pin money babysitting. When she had been unlucky enough to get kids who had been like him, little holy terrors, she earned every penny of her 10-cents an hour. She didn't understand Harry Antonelli. Never would and never will.

Dorothy shakes her head and says, "You teaching and coaching. Everyone's expectation but yours. I should have known you wouldn't be back in the fall. You hadn't signed your first teacher's contract because of its gross immorality clause. You made a joke of it saying that you couldn't sign in good conscience because it was a pledge not to do the things you enjoyed the most doing."

He laughs. It was no joke and she knew it. Obviously knows it now.

Harry came to Europe to sew wild oats too. In college, there'd been cheerleaders and sorority queens, abroad, the expectation of *Fräuleins* and *mademoiselles*. He'd been ready, willing and able for some gross immorality, which he found in quantity throughout his elongated European summer of 1938.

There are oats left in the bag, Harry thinks, but there is only one Dorothy Booth. She's one in a million. It's all so damn confusing.

They're standing closer, his doing or hers or both; the movement is too subtle to say. Harry smells perfume and perspiration, reminded of them on the back seat of her father's 1933 Chrysler Airflow, in his college freshman year and her high-school senior year, doors open, his oxford-clad feet hanging out, armrests killing his ankles, slacks bunched at his ankles, her saddle shoes around him, panties dangling from one foot.

The Airflow was a design failure and big loss of Chrysler's money and of her virginity, so she proclaimed. He was noncommittal, as it would ruin his self-image as a man/boy of the world. Letting her believe she was the net of many.

They were both lying.

Both, too, considered marriage a form of joint insanity.

Does she still?

Dorothy's hands come out and up, to block any move by the shifty halfback of years past. Damn, she could always read his mind, a talent that did their romance no good whatsoever.

"And you? Mother wrote that you graduated last year and taught this year."

"She's doing okay, by the way. Other than having a wart removed, she's in good health. Your dad and brother are doing well at your dad's auto body shop, though they're worried that if war starts for America, they won't be able to get parts, fenders and things. All the metal will go into tanks and guns."

Harry nods, as if he knows the latest on the home front. He's been meaning to get off a letter, he really and truly has.

"Tabby is alive and well and feisty," she says. "He's old. He must be ten or twelve. Tabby has those cracked-chinaware eyes now."

Tabby is Harry's cat, a short-haired gray tabby with sharp incisors and saw-tooth ears. Boys are supposed to like dogs, girls cats, and that was that. But thanks to Tabby's ferocious behavior, nobody questioned Harry's manhood. The kitty had slept on his bed every night since it wandered into their backyard eight or nine years ago, and subsequently sent half the cats and dogs in the neighborhood to the vet.

"Tabby is Harry and Harry is Tabby," Dorothy says. "I swear, you two are brothers."

He says, "Is he still frisky?"

"He is. Not long ago, a yippy-yappy poodle was taking a crap in your back yard and Tabby took offense. The owner's vet had it for three days."

"Poodles. The damn things are delicate. They shouldn't be running loose. They should be crapping in their own yards. Or all over the house."

"Once again, your mom had to stop your dad from taking Tabby for a ride. All those vet bills add up, he said, but she won that argument. Again."

"That's my kitty boy. Anyway, You did graduate from college last year. You wanted to teach high school."

Dorothy makes a face and says, "I've just finished teaching a year at Jefferson High. One long, long, long year. Home ec."

"Home ec?"

"I wanted to teach chemistry and physics."

"You were good at science, a lot better than me and most of the boys," Harry says.

"I was. I majored in both physical sciences in college, with a minor in metallurgy. Half the time the only girl in my classes. There was one opening to teach them at Jefferson and it was given to a guy. I could run circles around him in quantitative analysis, but chem and physics were quote-unquote unladylike. If I wanted a job there, I had to teach the other opening, home economics, teaching girls how to cook and sew, things they should be learning at home from their mothers. I was forced to be the advisor for the Homemaking Club too, which was more of the same, preparing them to be good little housewives. And to substitute in a girl's health class. I'd teach them about washing their hands and things, not the stuff they really need to know, if you catch my drift.

"I don't know if I'm going to sign a contract there for next year. I hated getting up every morning. On weekends, I took flying lessons and got my commercial license and flight instructor certification. I wanted to start an aviation club at school, but they nixed that too. A Piper J-3 Cub was too dangerous for girls."

"My Amelia Earhart," Harry says, moving into her upraised hands, which stiffen.

"Before I forget, Chuck sends his regards."

Saburo (Chuck) Taihotsu was Harry's best friend in high school, somebody else he'd lost touch with, also his fault.

Chuck was class valedictorian and the only guy in the all-city meet who was faster than Harry in the 100-yard dash, 10.1 seconds to Harry's 10.2. Chuck didn't gloat and Harry wasn't crestfallen. They were just happy that they were one and two, in whatever order.

"Great. How's he doing."

"Good and not so good. He's in his second year at Stanford med school, passing his classes with flying colors."

"That's swell. He'll make a great doctor. What's the 'not so good'?"

"Anti-Japanese feelings are building. Some people think that Japan might even go to war against us."

Harry shakes his head. "Japan's just a few little islands halfway around the world. They're acting crazy, but they're not that crazy."

Dorothy continues, "Chuck's been called names. Jap and Nip. It's on the verge of violent."

Harry shakes his head again. "They're screwy. Japan's Japanese are Nips and Japs. Loyal American Japanese like Chuck are Japanese Americans. Chuck didn't rape Nanking. If the Japs start a war with us, Chuck will be called a Jap or a Nip and there's nothing we can do about that, but the Japs are too smart to attack us. By and large, they're a sneaky nation, but they know enough to keep their mitts off of the United States of America."

Dorothy's head is spinning, trying to latch on to Harry's logic. She's angrier about behavior toward Chuck and with her teaching circumstances than with Harry, a man she knows too well. A man she too easily forgives.

She looks around and says, "May I ask, how are you supporting yourself?"

"May I ask, who *we* is?"

"I asked my question first."

"Not before I asked my first question first."

She looks at him, head cocked.

"And how come you're here, Dorothy? I don't think it's cuz you couldn't stand being away from me any longer. Not that I'm complaining, You are a sight for sore—"

"Harry."

"Well, I've been doing different things, keeping my choices open and variable, so I'm Johnny-on-the-spot when opportunities arise. I'm currently in the import-export business with some associates."

"Oh God, Harry, we all feared you were up to no good."

"Since when is the import-export profession up-to-no-good?"

"You're a smuggler and black marketeer, aren't you? I've read stories about that. It's rampant in Europe these days."

Harry rocks a hand, another tip to her that he's lying. He makes a mental note to keep his hands in his pockets when he lies to her.

"Not exactly. Black marketeering, as you incorrectly call it, isn't exactly a crime, not exactly. It's a necessary function of the European economy. Things are different over here and you can't believe everything you read. Things are in short supply and prices fluctuate crazily. Supply and demand, you know. The void must be filled. The laws are casual in some areas. People do what they gotta do."

"That was a thick hunk of baloney, Harry. Any way you slice it, you're a criminal."

Harry smiles. "Okay, if you insist on insulting me, I'm a petty criminal by your closed-minded definition, a minor criminal who wouldn't hurt a fly. Unless I have to."

Dorothy Booth sighs, at a loss for words.

He edges toward her. She doesn't backpedal, a good sign.

Harry hears brakes screech and car doors slam.

He runs to the hallway window. Under a bright streetlight, the two PVDE baby grands from the Canção are piling out of a mile-long Mercedes-Benz convertible.

With them is a Nordic type, a torpedo in a double-breasted suit with blonde hair and dead eyes. He's looking up at Harry, pointing and shouting in German, and a PVDE agent is shouting in Portuguese.

"Shit."

Dorothy's with him, peeking over his shoulder. "Who are they?"

"Whoever the hell they are, they're not Fuller Brush Men selling Girl Scout cookies."

"What were they yelling about?"

"I'm no linguist, but they sound like they want to have an unfriendly meeting with me."

"Why?"

"I haven't the foggiest notion."

They begin pounding on the front door.

"Friendly?"

"We have to scram out of here," Harry says.

"Harry, tell me, who are they?"

Harry has Dorothy by the hand, pulling her through an opposite hallway door than leads downstairs to the back street. "Portugal's secret police. A couple of birds I saw earlier today. Beyond that, I don't know."

"Harry."

The pounding is louder, accompanied by yelling.

The visitors kick the door in. Harry and Dorothy have made it to the second floor. He pulls her into the restroom and waits until the noise starts inside Harry's apartment

"There's a friend's dump where we can hide out," Harry says, meaning Peter Owen's.

Likely, it'll be vacant, Harry thinks, the occupant now preoccupied at PVDE Headquarters, Harry's address having been tortured out of him.

"I have a hotel room," Dorothy says.

"I like that better."

"Don't get any funny ideas."

"Let's amscray," Harry says. "We can work out those minor details later."

"Minor?"

"Come on. While they're inside, we can run for it."

They hurry down to the main floor, ignoring the landlady, who's out of her flat in her bathrobe, shaking her cigarette like a stick, yelling at Harry in Portuguese.

"What's she saying?"

"Happy July Fourth," Harry says, "If we can make it to the next block, we can lose them."

They run into the street.

The guy in the suit is not upstairs with the PVDE.

He's leaning against the Mercedes, pointing a Luger at them.

The sight of the pistol makes his legs wobbly, for Horatio Alger (Harry) Antonelli is afraid of only two things in the whole, wide world: guns and clowns.

"Those minor details," he tells Dorothy. "They'll have to come much later."

CHAPTER 4

Herr Dead Eyes directs them into the car with the barrel of his Luger, words of a universal language. Dorothy and Harry are scrunched in the back. The Mercedes-Benz convertible is a big car but not big enough. Harry is in the back-seat middle, a baby grand on his left, Dorothy pressed against the right door.

The other no-neck is driving, the Luger carrier in the front with him, the Luger at the ready but thankfully out of Harry's sight.

"If Goldilocks isn't Gestapo or SS, I'll eat my hat," Harry tells Dorothy out of the side of his mouth.

Then to the Aryan, "Hey, Fritz, you of the Indo-European master race."

No reply.

"Harry, don't antagonize him."

"He came out of the womb antagonized. Hey, Fritz, this isn't Berlin, you know. In case you haven't heard, Lisbon is neutral. Portugal is neutral. We're noncombatant civilians minding our own business. American citizens. What you're doing is illegal, you know. The Geneva Convention says so."

Same non-reaction.

Harry gives up.

They go into the heart of town, skirting the Praça do Comércio, the city's main plaza. Even from side streets, Dorothy and Harry can see that the Praça is inhabited by people out to beat the evening heat and by pigeons atop a heroic statue centering Comércio. They head to the Rio Tejo waterfront. The driver stops beside the river, behind ministry buildings shut down for the day. They are out of sight of the crowds.

The German jumps out of the car smartly and motions Harry out with his Luger and holds up his hand to Dorothy, signaling her to stay put.

"No," Harry says to her. "Go. Run for it. I'll keep them busy."

"Get out, Harry," she says, pushing him. "I'm a big girl. I'll be just fine. Go."

The Nazi walks Harry to the waterside, holsters the pistol inside his jacket, produces a pack of Chesterfields, and offers Harry one.

A last smoke before the blindfold goes on, Harry wonders?

Having no choice but to play the game, he accepts a cigarette and a flame from a lighter with a swastika on it. He glances at the car and sees that the PVDE goons have changed positions and are in the back, Dorothy between them. Other than that, they're behaving themselves. So far. If they try anything with Dorothy, he hopes he has the chance to come to her rescue, but first he has to rescue himself.

The German lights his own and takes a long drag, then holds it between thumb and forefinger like Peter Lorre in the movies. If this bird wants to talk about wine corks, he's out of luck too, Harry thinks. Whatever they've wrung out of Peter, the cork deal is a lost cause.

"My name is not Fritz, you lummox. Do you know what my name is?"

"I'm not a mind reader, Hans."

"Horst Wessel. Is that name familiar to you?"

"Oh yeah. It sure is," says Harry Antonelli. "I was a history major in college, but I didn't learn about that mug out of a schoolbook. He was a Brownshirt goon who was living with a whore. It was around nineteen-thirty or thirty-one. Wessel got into a beef with his landlady, which I can sympathize with. She sent for her Communist Party friends, who blew Wessel's face off when he answered the door. Goebbels made him into a martyr, complete with the Horst Wessel Song Wessel wrote himself, you and your Nazis' fucked-up answer to *America the Beautiful*. And don't hold your breath waiting for Bing Crosby or the Ink Spots to sing it either."

"You are badly misinformed. Being an American, this is understandable propaganda learned in your backward schools, designed for your nation of barefoot hillbillies. Horst Ludwig Georg Erich Wessel was an intellectual and a courageous soldier who sacrificed his life for the Third Reich. He was taken from us on the twenty-third of February in nineteen-thirty by degenerate communist subhumans."

Eyebrows raised, Harry says, "What would your countryman Sigmund Freud think about you taking Wessel's name? Him rising from the dead as you."

"Sigmund Freud is a Jew. You are an American, yes?"

"You know I am, Fritz. Take the wax out of your ears. Through and through, I'm red, white and blue."

"Why do you people resist and help the *Engländers*? We are on the brink of establishing the New Order in Europe today and tomorrow throughout the world. The *Führer* is the messiah. He cannot be stopped."

"He's not the first power-grubbing dictator who said that, Hans."

The Nazi holds a thumb and forefinger an eighth of an inch apart. "The greatest leader in the history of mankind, and I once sat this close to him."

Here in Lisbon, Harry wonders?

He says, "Wow. You sat that close to George Washington?"

Horst Wessel stares at him.

"Did I guess wrong? FDR? Abe Lincoln?"

Wessel doesn't even blink. Luger or no Luger, he's giving Harry the willies. All this cuckoo bird lacks is a monocle and a dueling scar. Harry would be happy to provide the gash.

As the staring continues, Wessel's eyes narrow.

"Are we having a moment of silence in honor of Wessel?" Harry says.

"Enjoy your warped humor while you can. The *Führer* will laugh last."

"Adolf the messiah? Are we gonna see pictures of Hitler with a halo," Harry says. "That'd be a sight, the halo slipping and sliding on top of his greasy mop."

The German snaps his fingers. "Stop the foolish talk. Show me your identification."

Encouraged by the Luger, Harry hands him his wallet and passport without protest, thinking that along with the needling, he's buying time. It is a decision he will later regret.

"Horatio Alger Antonelli," Wessel says.

"I was named for a fictional character who was underprivileged, yet became rich and famous by virtues of honesty, bravery, determination, correct moral conduct, perseverance and hard work."

Wessel gives Harry back his identification. "Are you an uptight man like him, this fictitious Horatio Alger?"

"No."

Wessel frowns. "You look Jewish to me, with your dark features and your nose. This nose of yours, it has a jagged Semitic curve."

"You oughta get your eyes checked. That's no curve. It's a pothole."

"Are you Jewish? Is Antonelli a Jew name?"

"It's Italian, as Italian as that blockhead Mussolini."

"Jewish and Italian too, a mongrelized mix? Explain."

Harry Antonelli's face fits in a category between ruggedly handsome and disfigured. Too much football, too many brawls. Have to get this schnoz fixed someday, Harry thinks. If only people would stop breaking it.

He says, "Only on my mother's and father's sides."

"You are then a part-Jew?"

Harry smiles. "I confess. I bumped off Jesus. Jesus, who was a Jew in his own right. Confused? So am I."

The Nazi squints. "Is that a joke?"

"You decide, Hans. Actually, really, I'm a lapsed Catholic. After my time in your Nazi Germany, I realized that there is no God. Even He doesn't have that ugly a sense of humor. Satan, maybe, inspired by a vicious hangover. Only the stinko prince could dream up Adolf Hitler and what he does."

"Horatio Alger, Jew boy, where is the gold?"

Peter Owen and his "figure of speech." Is there mythical gold that's real, El Dorado in a Lisbon neighborhood? Was Peter taken away because of money, a small-time swindle, not for mouthing off about local politics?

He severely doubts if this nutty Nazi is a man of metaphors and similes. Harry sneaks glances at the Mercedes-Benz, increasingly puzzled and increasingly concerned about Dorothy, who is shaking her head, protesting something.

"Gold? Stop the music, Fritz. You're not making any sense."

"I am not Fritz. No more Fritz and Hans out of your mouth. Our gold is missing."

"Hans and Fritz, *the Katzenjammer Kids*. Two wisenheimer kids who raise all sorts of hell. It's one of my favorite comics in the Sunday paper. That's where you belong, Hans Fritz. In the funny papers."

"If you wish to see your Engländer partner alive again, you will stop speaking nonsense and insults, and tell me about the gold."

Peter's kidnapping—confirmed.

"I don't know anything about any gold, Hans. I'd lie to you about gold if I knew about gold but I don't know a damn thing about a single, solitary ounce of gold. That's the honest-to-God no-fucking-bullshit truth."

"You are challenging my knowledge of your language."

"What did I say you don't understand?"

The reincarnated Horst Wessel jabs his cigarette at the car.

"Your lovely lady friend in the automobile, note that she is between my Portuguese companions now. Uncouth men with primal tastes."

"Call off your dogs, Hans. I mean it."

"Her wiggling and objecting to their attention is a ruse. Do not be deceived. She is enjoying herself, a vamp as you call that type of woman. An American whore who does not walk the streets is nevertheless a whore. You want to see her again as she is now, before she is used by those brutes, you will tell me where the gold is."

Harry sees her beginning to squirm and push and plead. He sees where their hands are, where he *can't* see them. He feels his face redden. If these assholes abuse Dorothy they'll have to go through him first, consequences be damned.

The Kraut is speaking in Erich von Stroheim English now, a broken record about gold. Harry figures that he can interrupt and lecture the German further on illegality and neutrality and the Geneva Convention, things he has no interest in, or he can try to get his goat, to make him flip his wig and go for his Luger.

If Harry makes his move now, while it's holstered, the Nazi would have it out first, quicker than the Lone Ranger, and he'll be dead. Dorothy too, after they have their fun with her.

The first lesson of street fighting is to hit first and hit hard. The Nazi lunatic is keeping his distance, not giving Harry that chance to throw a punch, so he has to improvise to make him fly off the handle.

"Hey, Fritz, excuse me. Have you heard the latest joke?"

"Speak to me of the gold. I am out of patience with you, Horatio Antonelli."

"The gold can wait for a minute, Hans. Listen. I have a great gag for you, a million laughs. You know the definition of an Aryan superman?"

Wessel doesn't respond.

"He's as blond as Hitler, as slim as Goring, a greedy, bemedaled pig, and as tall as Goebbels, a clubfooted dwarf who screams his propaganda over the radio like a demented magpie."

Harry then forces a laugh.

The German tenses and flicks aside his cigarette. He doesn't laugh.

"Okay, Hans, here's more words of wisdom. You know why you Nazis hate Jews? Because they're smarter than you are and they'll be around long after you're gone, you and your thousand-year Reich that'll be lucky to last a thousand days."

He hesitates.

The German's eyes are like bulbs in a machine.

"You know the real reason Hitler's never married? Ever see him in Berlin with a dame on his arm? Him and his stupid mustache that looks like a filthy toothbrush. Being the boss, he should have no shortage of hot tomatoes. Like a Hollywood movie star.

"You know why he doesn't? Be honest, you do, you and everybody else does, but nobody can say it out loud. It's not because he's married to Germany like he claims. That's bullshit. It's because he doesn't like girls. Your *Führer's* a fairy, a swish, a pansy, a homo."

Bingo.

Harry has gone too far with his blasphemy, exactly what he wants. Herr Wessel reaches into his jacket, taking his eyes off Harry for an eyeblink. Harry lunges and catches his wrist when Wessel comes out with the Luger.

Harry grabs his other wrist. They began a jerky boogie-woogie without music or affection. The German's stronger than he looks, slowly gaining an advantage, moving his arms, bringing the barrel of the pistol around to Harry's head.

Harry's football instincts come back to him. He wrenches the Luger hand forward. It brushes his shoulder and goes off. Dorothy screams and a PVDE thug howls. Harry ducks and drives his other shoulder into Horst Wessel's midsection as if he were a tackling dummy.

The air goes out of the Nazi with a loud *whoomph*. The Aryan superman is losing his grip on the pistol. Harry peels his fingers back and takes it. He shoves the barrel against the German's collarbone, encouraging him to backpedal until, with a helpful shove, he splashes into the Rio Tejo.

As the German flails and coughs, Dorothy climbs out of the car and hurries to Harry, who aims the gun, freezing the pursuing PVDE agents in mid-step. One raises his hands straight up. His companion is stooped and raises just one, the other covering his crotch.

"Into the drink, boys. Gotta help your friend. Looks like they didn't give swimming lessons at Hitler Youth camp."

The agents move toward the edge, in no great hurry, one still moving like the Hunchback of Notre-Dame, clutching himself, in obvious pain.

"What's the matter, Hopalong?"

"I do not swim well, sir. Do not do this," he says in passable English.

"Sorry, champ. I no speak Portuguese."

Coughing and spitting and splashing, Horst Wessel yells, "You will pay dearly for this, Antonelli."

"I'm no sniper, boys, but I can't miss from this range," he says, one hand on the barrel, the other on the handle as he aims in the general direction of the Portuguese agents.

They hold their noses and jump in.

"Wait," Harry tells Dorothy as she begins to run toward the plaza. "Just to be safe, I'll shoot out a tire."

He fully realizes now what he has in his hand, a *gun*, every hard metallic edge of it a rattlesnake's fang.

"Harry, be careful. It's not a red-hot potato."

"Says you."

"Hang on to it and grip it the right way before you hurt somebody, for God's sake. When it went off while I was in the car, I heard the bullet zing barely over our heads."

"That was Fritz, not me."

There is more yelling in the river. The splashing sounds like kids in a wading pool, sans laughter.

"Harry, please hurry."

Harry tries to hang on and aim, but the terrifying firearm is a squirming, writhing viper. Eyes clenched shut, he shoots at a tire and hits the fuel tank instead. A stream of gasoline on the pavement ignites.

"The sights are off," Harry says, flinging the Luger into the river, where the threesome is attempting to tread water to the dock.

He takes her hand. "Be casual."

Around the corner of the ministry buildings, hand in hand, lovers out for an evening stroll, Dorothy tugs on him. "Slow down and be casual."

Harry pauses at the statue in the center of the Praça do Comércio, a man on horseback.

He points upward and says, "That's King José I. He was king during the 1755 earthquake. He got a lot of credit for restoring things, but it was his right-hand man, the Marquês de Pombal, who actually ran the show. It's a very long story."

"Harry, my history major," Dorothy says, kissing his cheek.

The flames and smoke from the gasoline are visible above the government buildings. When the car explodes, people duck and run for it. Pigeons that had been building guano epaulets on King José's shoulders fly off.

As they walk under the triumphal arch leading out of the Praça, Dorothy says, "There's our fireworks, Harry. Happy July Fourth."

CHAPTER 5

B attling his nerves, talking a mile a minute, Harry continues his history lecture:

From demolished 1755 Lisbon, the Marquês de Pombal built an entirely new city center, he tells Dorothy. Using a grid layout of streets, he linked the waterfront's Praça de Comércio with Rossio Square to the north. The buildings were semi-uniform and neo-Classical. It was Europe's first grid system, quite a deviation from impromptu layouts that on a map resembled week-old spaghetti. There were a number of heroic statues of the Pombal fella in town, and Harry figures he deserved them as much as anyone else.

This district is called Baixa (pronounced bay-sha), and Baixa is where Dorothy and Harry are, at a café on a side street, shielded by three and four-story buildings, out of sight of the riverfront and Harry's handiwork. The flames are gone as are the majority of the curious, but black smoke continues to rise and diffuse. They are within earshot of the sirens that have finally fallen silent. Thanks to Harry Antonelli, there is disorder in an area that passes for order in 1940 Lisbon.

Dorothy is having a small coffee, an *uma bica,* and a round egg-tart pastry, a local delicacy known as a *pastel de nata.* These are among the many unrationed treats in Europe's new City of Light.

"You have a knack for teaching history, if you'd please slow down and catch your breath," Dorothy says.

"Not teaching in a classroom. Only on field trips like this."

She says, "Teaching history while you modify it."

Harry's nerves are steadying, thanks to cigarettes and beer, his second Super Bock, a local brew.

"Dorothy, did you do something to make that goon howl and limp?"

"I did, by giving him a little squeeze."

"Um, did you give him a little squeeze where I think you little-squeezed him?"

"And twisted him too. He was unzipped and had it out. I didn't have to understand Portuguese to understand what he was saying he was going to do with it once he tore my clothes off. He was asking for it," Dorothy says. "You men, your brains are there."

Harry shivers, thinking that no squeeze in that region of the anatomy is a *little* squeeze.

"I'm not debating that one with you."

"I overheard the crazy Jew-hating rant by your Nazi friend. You haven't converted to Judaism, have you? Your mother had to drag you kicking and screaming to Mass. If you have converted, I'm not criticizing."

"I think conversion to Judaism is automatic after you've beaten up twenty-five Nazis. I've almost qualified. I should have drowned the son of a bitch. That'd count as double points."

She smiles. "That is so mean of you."

Harry tells her about his experience at *Kristallnacht*. "I have dreams where I'm walking on broken glass. Barefoot. These Nazis are creatures, Dorothy. They've turned their population into animals. I don't know how else to put it. They're the most modern in the world at war too. That blitzkrieg of theirs. Who knows what else they have up their sleeves."

"Harry, up on your soapbox, you're as red as a beet. I didn't know you had a political bone in your body."

"I do when ten Nazi fanatics try to stomp me into a grease spot," he says.

"Ten?"

"I was busy flooring the bastards. I wasn't counting."

"Did I overhear that creepy crawly Nazi demand gold from you?"

"Yeah, you did. Gold is a bulletin to me."

Dorothy looks at him.

"Really."

She raises her eyebrows.

"I can tell the truth once in a while, you know, and I'd sure remember gold."

"Because of those grunting Neanderthals, I didn't hear everything. Did he ask you about tungsten too?"

He stares at her. "Where did that come from?"

She sips her espresso.

"You pulled 'tungsten' out of the clear blue sky, Dorothy. Wessel didn't mention tungsten," he says, recalling Peter's cryptic comment on it.

She says, "Not actually out of the clear blue sky. We have some other topics too we need to cover, you and I, to be perfectly honest."

"There's that *we* again," Harry says, leaning forward. "You turning up at my dump too. Nature abhors a coincidence, you know."

"Doesn't nature abhor a vacuum?"

"I'm speaking of history. I don't know anything about science and vacuums. I never got above a B-minus in a science or math class. That's your field. In case you haven't heard, Lisbon is a playpen for MI6, the SS, and the Gestapo. And American spies, neutral noncombatants with nothing better to do. Training for the war that we're itching to get into, if you believe some. Everybody's spying on everybody else and making money selling information to each other whether it's bushwa or not. Some spies are good at it. Others are conspicuously inconspicuous. There are more stool pigeons in this town than pigeons on heroic statues. Any time you come across a journalist, watch out."

"Why?"

"Half of them are secret agents. They can ask rude, demanding questions without being suspected by playing dumb, which some of them are."

"Is that what your English friend, Mr. Peter Owen, does for a living? Is he a stringer for British papers?" Dorothy says, then taking a bite of her *pastel de nata*. "This is absolutely delicious, Harry. I've never had anything like it."

Harry chokes on his beer. Dorothy jumps up and slaps his back.

When he stops coughing, he says, "Out with it, Dorothy. What the hell is going on, you turning up here on my doorstep? You and your *we*, blindsiding me with Peter. If this is football, you'd be flagged for fifteen yards."

"Your doorstep," she says, sighing.

"Speaking of which. We can go back there and discuss it in private."

She says, bending a permanent-wave curl, "In case you have any ideas about you and me, forget it."

"Who, me?" he says, stroking her arm.

"Not so fast, buster. I have a confession to make. In London, I had and have a whirlwind romance going with a dashing British Spitfire pilot. He's already shot down four *Messerschmitt* fighters. He's the bravest man I've ever known."

"I guess tossing a Nazi in the drink doesn't count for much compared to that. On top of beating up twelve Nazis during *Kristallnacht*," says a deflated Harry, thinking that her Spitfire deadeye probably isn't afraid of guns or clowns. Certainly not clowns.

She replies by sipping her coffee.

Harry says, "Horst Wessel falsely accused me of having an English partner, but not by name."

"This is wonderful coffee, Harry, superior to any I've ever tasted at home."

Harry studies her. There's something different about Dorothy Booth, not her appearance, but something deeper, how she talks, how she carries herself. She's always been independent, speaking her mind, but now it was beyond that. She's acting like a—suffragette.

Whether it's her intention or not, she's validated the fact that he's wasted the last two years, bumming around Europe. Much of the time spent in Lisbon isn't entirely due to his fascination with it, but because it was his last stop before heading home to begin life as an adult. Adulthood is nipping at his heels and he's losing ground.

Dorothy also studies Harry. She's almost but not quite sorry that she broke the news about her romance in England. Almost. Harry does wear his heart on his sleeve. Regardless of his shenanigans, he is to her an imperfect Jack Armstrong, the all-American boy. The little kid who tore into playground bullies and gained inspiration from heroes in comic strips.

"Wait. Didn't you say you came in on the Clipper? It comes from the Azores, not London."

"That was an earlier trip, Harry."

"For the hundredth time, who the hell is *we*?"

She gently puts down her cup, stands up, and brushes her skirt.

"Harry, please hail a taxi and escort me home. It's close by, but under the circumstances, let's not walk and be moving targets."

CHAPTER 6

"Husband? Boyfriend? Your Spitfire fighter pilot? Is this who your *we* is? If your flyboy is shooting down Germans, he's sure as hell not doing it from Lisbon," says an unreasonably jealous Harry Antonelli.

"Peter Owen, your friend, is he suitable company you should be keeping?"

"I ask a reasonable question and this is how you answer. Whether Peter's a friend or an acquaintance, that's the sixty-four dollar question, is it? And what's he got to do with the price of tea in China?"

"Driver, please slow down," Dorothy says, leaning forward.

They are lurching, slowing and speeding, slowing and speeding, in a taxi that is seemingly wider than some of the streets, miraculously avoiding pedestrians and harder objects such as lampposts and buildings. Headlight pods mounted on the fenders are misaimed, cockeyed, loose and cross-eyed, essentially useless. That downtown Lisbon is lively day and night provides illumination that has saved the lives of many taxicab passengers.

"Do you think this cabdriver speaks English, Harry? I know he heard me."

"If he does, he's pretending not to. Everybody in the world speaks a foreign language but us bloody Yanks, as my missing English friend or acquaintance, Peter Owen, calls us. *Our* missing mutual friend or acquaintance. This is a good time to talk about him."

"Is he genuinely missing?"

59

"Don't play dumb, Dorothy."

"Harry, that's absurd."

"The past four hours have been absurd."

"There, on our left. That man with the cart we almost sideswiped and killed, what's he roasting?"

"Chestnuts. Hey, you told the driver the Hotel Metropole," Harry says. "Did I hear you right?"

"You did."

"Okay, well, he is headed in that direction. You have a room there?"

"We do."

Harry whistles. He had drank at the outside Metropole bar, under an umbrella, nursing a beer that was too rich for his blood, let alone a room. Old and swank, on Rossio Square, every room has a view worth seeing, from the square itself to the high-and-mighty *Castelo de São Jorge.*

"Dorothy, people are double-bunked in cubbyholes in slums, and you have a room at one of the swellest hotels in town."

"We do."

The cab stops in front of the hotel, hard, by the Column of Don Pedro IV, the first emperor of Brazil, who is balanced atop it on horseback, centering the Rossio (pronounced row-see-oh). Street lighting casts the profile of the nineteenth century hero onto them.

Harry says, "The Metropole is crawling with Germans, you know. They're like cockroaches in this joint."

"So we've heard. You can come up for a nightcap if you'd like, Harry."

"Yeah, I'd like, but isn't three a crowd? You and me and this secret *we* of yours."

"My mysterious third party hasn't arrived yet, so I'll be alone until tomorrow."

"Yeah?" Harry says, paying the driver.

"Don't get any ideas, buster."

"I wouldn't dream of getting out of line," Harry lies as a uniformed doorman rushes to open their front doors.

Hotel staffers greet Dorothy warmly and give Harry the evil eye, something he's accustomed to.

"Half the hired help is on Berlin's payroll too. All they're missing is swastika armbands," Harry mutters as they go from a marble lobby up marble stairs to the third floor. Dorothy unlocks the door of not a room but a suite.

"Holy cow," Harry says, gawking.

It has to cost 250 escudos a night—$10! More than most Portuguese earn in a month. The average worker in Lisbon makes 70¢ a day.

"It's been a long, long day," Dorothy says by way of explanation, tossing her purse on a table and giving him a peck of the cheek. "Help yourself to a nightcap for me too."

Harry shakes out a Camel and sticks it in his mouth.

"Please don't smoke. They're stinky and they bother my sinuses."

"What bothered sinuses? Haven't you seen the advertising in the magazines? This is the brand more doctors smoke than any other cigarette. Next thing you'll say, they're bad for you."

"You're an adult, Harry. In years. You decide about your health. But not in this room. Oh, before I forget, here. I know how much you like the funny papers, the world-beater heroic ones the best. Here's a brand-new strip you may not have seen before."

"You make it sound like I'm a kid who didn't grow up. I don't buy comic books. I just read the funnies to relax."

"I'm not debating that subject or any other with you. It's yet another debate nobody can win."

She hands him a folded page from her purse. With that she goes into a bedroom, closes the door, and, *goddamn*, latches it.

He'd been rehearsing to tell Dorothy that he'd stopped writing her for her own good, so she'd feel free to find a good man, marry, have children, a dog and a cat, and marigolds in their back yard. Inside their white picket fence. It's only a partial lie.

Whoever the lucky guy is, the limey flyboy son of a bitch, Harry is green with jealousy, but not enough to drop on one knee and offer her a ring.

He has decided to discard the plan and say nothing. She'd see right through him. And gotten steamed in the process.

He takes a closer look around. The sitting room is right out of a Victorian novel, the decor sickeningly overdone. Turkish carpets, flocked wallpaper, spindly chairs and tables with curlicue legs. And to top it off, a framed picture of Brits on horseback, chasing some pitiful fox that's never done them an ounce of harm.

The room reminds him sourly of the era he had to study preparatory to his history degree, two five-credit classes worth of misery. In the textbooks, everybody in those times behaved themselves with the opposite sex, but Harry knows better. The hoop skirts and knickers must've been a challenge, but people were people. Guys always found a way.

He unfolds her gift to him, a full-color Sunday comics page. It is new to him. *Wonder Woman*, a hot dame wearing patriotic tights of blue with white stars. Her top is red, not much left to the imagination.

Reading along, he sees that she's as tough and talented as any male superhero, Captain Marvel or any of them except maybe Superman. Wonder Woman has bracelets that deflect bullets, a good kind of jewelry to have, and an invisible airplane at her disposal. It looks faster that a Messerschmitt or Spitfire or anything else in the air.

A magic lasso too. When she ropes you and pulls you in close and questions you, you've got no choice but to tell the truth. Her and I and that polygraph lariat, Harry thinks, we'd never hit it off.

HISTORICAL NOTE: Wonder Woman wasn't introduced until December 1941, but Dorothy has ignored the chronological anomaly, feeling that Harry needs to welcome a sexual fetish into his fantasy world. Buck Rogers' Wilma Deering and Flash Gordon's Dale Arden are already spoken for and she suspects that the sexual preference *of Dick Tracy's Tess Trueheart is unclear, too complex or lurid for the comic pages.*

Wonder Woman doesn't have a favorite fella; her relationship with Colonel Steve Trevor is platonic, although he wishes it weren't. Harry likes nothing more than a great figure and a challenge.

After two or three readings,. Harry sets it aside, thinking that Dorothy has that magical power over him without a lasso. *Wonder Woman* is giving him uncomfortable urges, a sick fantasy of getting into her make-believe, star-spangled britches.

He recalls Mr. Harrison, his ninth-grade boys' health teacher. Mr. Harrison talked about stuff that wasn't in the textbooks, like what coaches told you not to do on the eve of a game. What they'd say made you go blind and grow hair on the palms of your hands. Mr. Harrison said that was bunk. Mary FiveFingers was your best gal. Mary was there for you whenever you needed her and she never cheated on you or said that she had a headache or that she wasn't that kind of girl.

Mr. Harrison didn't return at the start of his sophomore year, and wasn't seen or heard from again. One rumor was that he'd been canned for how he talked in class. Another was him and the vice-principal's wife. The rumor Harry believed was his breath. Mr. Harrison chewed Doublemint all day long, despite gum-chewing being against the rules for the kids. Harry knew that Mr. Harrison chewed Doublemint to hide the smell of his breakfast whiskey, but all it did was make his breath smell like a mint julep.

In an effort to take his mind off sweet Mary merging with Wonder Woman, he uses his super-power observation skills to find inside a small icebox a good supply beer and wine.

Super Bock in hand, he looks out the window at the plaza, still abuzz at the late hour, but he quickly closes the drapes. All the Krauts in and around the Metropole, who knows who's looking back at him?

Harry goes through more beer and wine. Thinking that the other half of the *we* couldn't be a *he*, her dashing RAF ace or anyone else, or he sure as hell wouldn't have been invited into the room. Some solace there, he thought, staring at her locked door that might as well be a bank vault.

Maybe a teacher friend from Dorothy's school. If so, Harry wonders what she looks like. Wonders if she'd be any friendlier than Dorothy.

Dying for a smoke and exhausted, ready to turn in, he tries the other bedroom door. Also locked.

The sofa with its flowery padding and ornamental wood is built for a maiden aunt and her poodle. It's the choice of that or a wooden floor and throw rugs.

Harry curls up on the sofa, hoping the alcohol will allow him to blot out the day's events, all the trouble he's in on top of the trouble he's already been in, and let him sleep tight.

It doesn't.

Where's Peter?

Who is *we*?

Harry wonders if he can find a Wonder Woman costume Dorothy's size and persuade her to wear it.

He eventually gets to sleep and has a cavalcade of nightmares. In the worst, Dorothy is hovering in midair over him like a dragonfly while he's being carried off the football field, Coach is in his ear next to the stretcher saying that someday they'd make helmets that are stronger than leather, like out of aluminum or stainless steel.

Crazy.

CHAPTER 7

Harry is violently aroused by a slamming door and hands coming together by his face like thunder. He doesn't know who or what it is, but he does know it isn't applause.

"Up and at 'em, Antonelli. A new day is dawning and room service is bringing up our eggs. Nourishment for the mission ahead."

Shit, Harry thinks, in the fetal position on the torturous couch, as he bends tighter and covers his ears.

The clapping is louder. "Not next week, Antonelli. Time's a'wasting."

Unfortunately, Harry recognizes the voice of his tormenter. He turns and opens his eyes. The other half of the "we" looming above him is Dorothy's big brother, David (Don't Call Me Dave) Booth. He should have known.

Dave Booth became *David* Booth in the third grade, a year ahead of Harry, when he brought home a report card filled with stick-on gold stars. Harry hadn't seen it, but he knew Booth had looked at himself in the mirror holding up the card. I am so special. I am *David*, not Dave.

Dave/David Booth had gone through high school, college and grad school, lickety-split, brainier than most of the teachers and professors, leaving a thick shiny glow of gold stars trailing from his Phi Beta Kappa key like moondust.

The last Harry heard, Booth went to work for a hush-hush government agency right after college. Dorothy had told Harry that days before he left for his summer in Europe. She didn't know who he'd gone to work for, or said she didn't.

David Booth is tall and wiry, an all-city basketball player in high school, so he wasn't just a grind. David had always believed that Dorothy was too good for Harry. While this is true, big brother's smug certainty about that and most all else irks the hell out of Harry. The son of a bitch believes that he knows everything and, worse, he hasn't often been proven wrong.

Harry slowly coaxes himself to a sitting position. Dorothy is out of her locked bedroom in a bathrobe. Looking at her while speaking to David, he says, "Let me guess. You were enjoying a good night's sleep somewhere while Dorothy was out reeling me in."

"Reeling. I object to that term," Dorothy says.

David says, "Believe it or not, I arrived here after you last night. Dorothy and I came together on the Clipper, but I had business to tend to. I must say, even with the turbulence, riding in that Clipper was not as harrowing as being in a Lisbon taxi. I'm told that you two had quite an adventure."

"Not my fault."

"It never is your fault," David says. "Whatever it is."

"You were quiet as a mouse when you came in, David."

"You were comatose, Harry. I could have brought along a brass band."

With a chin out to there and Dorothy's intelligent eyes, David Booth is neither pretty nor handsome. David is – how should I describe him, Harry thinks? – aristocratic. Has been since the third grade, maybe with a constellation of gold stars, perhaps emerging from the womb with a jutting jaw.

He says, "What the hell are you doing here? You and you. Don't tell me that my parents sent you to check up on me."

David says, "Your mother, who you write once in a blue moon, needs someone to check up on you, but that's not us. We didn't travel all this distance to babysit."

Harry has no answer.

David Booth says, "You managed to get my sis into trouble before she was in Lisbon for less than twenty-four hours, placing her in extreme jeopardy."

Dorothy shakes her head. "David, please."

"It wasn't my doing and you'd be proud of her. She handled those fascist thugs very well. Believe me, I wouldn't've survived without her."

Dorothy blushes. Harry wonders if she'd given her brother all the details of her part in the foray. As far as Harry is concerned, David's biggest fault is being a prude.

"Nothing is ever your doing, Harry."

"It wasn't his fault this time, David," Dorothy says. "Not all his fault."

Harry looks at David. "There you are. They asked for swimming lessons. The sights on the Luger the crazy Nazi tried to knock me off with were haywire, so the gas tank going kablooey, it was just one of those things."

"Let's move ahead, shall we?"

"I'm not complaining if we do, wherever we're going. How did you find me, use a bloodhound?"

"You left an easy trail, like bread crumbs, throughout your odyssey across Europe via complaints to the United States Embassies in Belgium, Denmark, Hungary, Italy, Czechoslovakia, France, Spain, and, before we severed diplomatic relations, Germany. Your last postcard home, yellowed with age, had a photo of a famous Lisbon sight on it. The Tower of Belém, I believe."

"I won't claim that everything bad said about me wasn't true, but there were extenuating circumstances. Language misunderstandings. Politics."

"Street brawling and petty crime are extenuating?"

"I've reformed if in fact the allegations against me are even true, which they aren't, so there's no need for me to reform. You're being fed a line."

David says, "In Budapest, that countess."

An elegant lady a few years his senior named Magda, who he had met in the bar of an elegant hotel, an elegant lady who didn't fit the prim, conventional definition of a lady.

"She said she was a countess. I had serious doubts. Anybody could see that her jewelry was fake."

"Her husband challenged you to a duel, so goes the story."

"I had serious doubts that he was a count. He refused to tell Magda his source of income."

"Pistols, was it? Or your choice of epee or saber?"

"I did the smart, cowardly thing and scrammed."

"In his car."

"How'm I going to walk thirty miles?"

"You jimmied the ignition."

"I didn't steal it. I borrowed it and left it at the border not too badly damaged. Anyway, he was a Nazi."

"Belgium."

"Like Denmark, I had to get a wiggle on to keep one step ahead of the Krauts. I was too busy staying out of trouble to cause trouble."

"Madrid."

"They won that civil war of theirs and acted like they'd won the Rose Bowl. It was impossible to say the right thing to anybody. According to Franco, there was a Russian-financed and trained communist under every bush."

HISTORICAL NOTE: Francisco Franco used the threat of international communism as justification for every abuse and atrocity from the 1937 bombing of Guernica to the end of him in 1975.

The Booth siblings look at each other, then at Harry.

David says, "Complaints from the Portuguese foreign ministry to the British Embassy here in Lisbon are exceptionally egregious.

They came from people complaining about shady business practices perpetrated by you and your partner, a Mr. Peter Owen."

Harry looks at Dorothy. "You did inform big brother that he's been kidnapped by the PVDE?"

She shrugs. "I did say that it was possible."

Harry groans.

"The British disavow any knowledge of him or that your Mr. Peter Owen is even an English citizen."

"Well, that's Peter for you. Add me to the disavowal list."

"Smoothing things over with them will be one of my least pleasant duties."

"Your duties in what capacity?" Harry says.

"What is this about gold and tungsten, Harry?"

"If I knew where a bunch of gold was, I'd be in sunny Rio with it. On the beach, drinking those drinks they put fruit and umbrellas in. As far as tungsten is concerned, why does tungsten keep coming up? Tungsten is none of my concern."

"I don't doubt the Rio part for a minute. You may not enjoy seeing me, Harry," David says. "You never do, but the secret police is after you now, thanks to the skirmish at the riverfront, the car explosion, and God knows what else. You need me."

Harry's hangover intensifies. His skull is squeezing, as if in a vice.

Looking downward, head in hands. "I need you?"

"You do."

"I repeat, David, what the hell are you doing here?"

"I'm a wholesale appliance salesman looking to expand in southern Europe," David says. "That is my pretext and all I can say."

Harry looks at him and laughs. "Swell. What brands? Westinghouse, GE? The same models sold in Corn Tassel, Nebraska?"

David glares at him.

"Whoever your spy bosses are, they haven't done their homework. Selling one-ten electricity stoves and things to people on two-twenty juice who can't afford them? Nobody will buy your bushwa for a second. Whose brainstorm was that?"

David ignores Harry's criticism. "I will let you in on a little secret, as much as I'm permitted to."

Harry interrupts with raised arms and whispers,"Let's put the brakes on for a minute. This hotel is infested with Krauts. You know, they make microphones these days so small you can hide them in a light socket."

David says, "But we have to talk and there's no time to waste."

David's melodrama is making Harry's head throb.

"Time out," Harry says, jabbing fingertips to a palm.

He gingerly finds his feet and goes around the room testing light switches. The one by the coat closet doesn't work. He unscrews it with a coin. Inside is a box twice the size of a pack of cigarettes with vertical slots in front.

"Oh," David says, the shortest answer Harry remembers him ever giving to anything.

"Leave it there," Harry goes to him and whispers. "If they don't know we discovered it, they'll believe anything we say that we want them to know."

Then he says in a normal voice, thinking of Dr. Huer, Buck Rogers' friend and genius inventor, "David, it's great you have the invisibility ray perfected and here for testing. If it works like it did in the lab, we can spy on whoever we want."

He winks at Dorothy.

Then winks at David.

Dorothy smiles and returns the wink.

David rolls his eyes.

There's a knock on the door.

Harry runs to the window and looks between the curtains and down, gauging how far below the ground is.

David says, "Please calm down, Harry. I trust that the authorities haven't traced you here. Not yet."

"Breakfast," Dorothy says, opening the door to a waiter and a cart.

"I can't look an egg in the yolk," Harry says.

"Breakfast is the most important meal of the day, Antonelli," Dorothy says as she steps aside for the waiter and cart. "I teach my gals that in home ec."

Harry aims himself in the direction of the bathroom.

"While you're having breakfast, give me a few minutes to powder my nose, then we can talk. I know just the place. You can beat your gums all you want there."

CHAPTER 8

In a taxi, Harry narrates their trip, pointing out historic buildings and a hole in the wall that serves, in his estimation, the best Chinese food in town. He gives the *Sé*, the city's cathedral, special attention.

"It was built in 1150 and restored after the 1755 earthquake and three earlier shakers. The twin castellated gray bell towers are unusual."

Dorothy says, "Harry Antonelli, our historian, travel guide, and polymath. Do you attend mass there?"

Harry laughs.

David snorts.

Dorothy says, "Your mother wouldn't be surprised that you don't."

After the third taxi change, up and down two hills, Dorothy says, "We passed four churches besides that cathedral."

Tapping the briefcase on his lap, David says, skeptically, "In spite of your antics, I suppose all these precautions are necessary."

"For me, yeah. Many things don't work right here, but the PVDE, the secret police are on the ball—them and their Nazi pals like the nut I gave swimming lessons to. For you, a commercial appliance salesman who knows all about my problems over here, you tell me if this is necessary. Being a spy and secret agent, David, you of all people know that the precautions are necessary. You and the agency who sent you. What agency is it? You probably told me but I forgot."

"Digging will do you no good, Harry. I am a commercial appliance salesman and you are—whatever you are, not authorized for classified information."

Dorothy says, "Harry is a living, breathing, unauthorized cliffhanger, David."

Harry turns around and says, "Speaking of cliffhangers. You guys, do you remember when we were kids, on Saturdays we'd walk to the Columbia City Theatre and spend a dime to see Tom Mix? There'd be a cartoon, a newsreel and a serial. I loved the serials the most. Tarzan, Flash Gordon. They'd end with cliffhangers you'd never think they'd survive, but they did. Next Saturday, you'd see how. Flash on the Planet Mongo dealing with Ming the Merciless, that was the scariest. As nutty as Europe is these days, they're on my mind a lot."

"You continue to inhabit that make-believe world of yours," David says. "A man in his twenties."

"These days, is that so bad, to escape once in a while? Stick around Lisbon awhile. You'll find out."

"You and your cartoons," Dorothy adds. "There is a limit."

"You guys are piling on. That's a fifteen-yard penalty."

She smiles and taps his shoulder. "How did you like the '*Wonder Woman*' strip I gave you?"

Harry whistles. "Did you bring an outfit like that with you?"

She laughs.

Her brother glares at her, then him.

"If I can find one, would you wear it?"

"You'll never change, Harry, never in a million years."

"You can tie me up with the magic lasso."

She cuffs him gently on an ear.

"But I'll still lie through my teeth."

"You're sick, Antonelli," David says.

"I know."

Dorothy says, "Harry, for as much as you loved the movies,

I'll never forget the phony excuse you made when I got the circus tickets that time. You've never told me why."

They were in high school then, he recalls. The senior Booth had repaired Harry's football-damaged choppers free of charge, providing he treated his daughter with respect. Harry lived up to his end of the bargain, but not in the way her father preferred. But that's another story.

Dr. Booth had been given the circus tickets by a dental supply salesman. Circuses invariably had clowns, so Harry developed a stomach ache that day.

He says, "It's not a phony excuse. I ate green apples off a neighbor's tree and got a belly ache."

"There were no apple trees within five blocks of us," Dorothy says.

"It could've been an under-ripe pear. It's been so long, how am I supposed to remember?"

David says, "Let's keep on the beam, shall we? This isn't the comics or movies. This is real life, no circuses, no cartoons."

Harry says, "Yeah? Brother and sister Booth off to summer camp in Europe. Is that real life? Not in my book."

He waits for a retort, but doesn't receive it.

"I'll give you a week in Lisbon and you tell me if *this* is real life."

Harry directs the taxi to stop in the middle of a steep Alfama street, three blocks from his flat.

"Pay the man, David," Harry says. "It's on Uncle Sam, right?"

As David does, muttering to himself, Dorothy says, "I wouldn't like to be here at night wandering around."

"Even with the politics and the snooping, Lisbon's much safer than New York and even Seattle," Harry says defensively.

"You're leading us into an alley," David says. "Where are you taking us?"

"It's a street, not an alley."

"If you say so," David says.

"Sorry, Dave. We're a long way from Los Angeles," Harry says.

"Four-lane boulevards are in short supply."

Harry stops, looks around, then puts his shoulder to the door of a windowless unnamed and unnumbered building that has plaster missing in patches, as if it had been used for artillery practice. He does so again.

After a squeak and a crack, it opens.

"Wasn't it locked?" Dorothy says.

Harry answers by motioning them to follow him upstairs. Every step on the three stories of stairwell creaks precariously. Apartment occupants are either gone or sleeping it off.

Dorothy says, "Oh my gosh, Harry. This building smells worse than yours. Where on earth are you leading us?"

"The Black Hole of Calcutta?" David says.

"With all the refugees flooding in, there's a shortage of housing, you know," Harry snaps. "Weren't you briefed by Westinghouse or GE or whoever?"

"My my," David says. "Are you with Lisbon's chamber of commerce?"

"Please, Harry, where are we going?" Dorothy says.

"To Peter Owen's. If the PVDE has him, they won't be expecting him to be home."

David Booth laughs. "Harry, I have to love your logic. It's remarkable."

"Yeah? I didn't learn it during five years of grad school."

"Children, children," Dorothy says.

Peter Owens' door is locked too.

Harry rams a shoulder into it, pretending it's a USC linebacker. The door doesn't budge.

"Ouch goddamnit. Dorothy, can you spare a bobby pin?"

"Oh, Harry," she says. "Where did you learn to do this?"

A girlfriend in Amsterdam who supplemented her income as a clerk in a millinery shop as a burglar, he doesn't say.

"Dorothy? Come on. We haven't got all day."

She sighs heavily, digs into her purse, and slaps one into his hand.

"Don't tell Mother or Father," he says as he crouches, squinting at the keyhole.

As he searches for tumblers, Harry is thinking what a disappointment he's been to his parents. He'd been named Horatio Alger at his mother's insistence, known from an early age as Harry by everyone else. He'd been the only member of his family to attend college, let alone graduate.

He had spent four long years at the University of Washington in hometown Seattle, and couldn't have done so during the Depression without washing dishes at the dorm, getting free tuition for playing football, and working at his father's body and fender shop in the summers alongside older brother Lou, who will rightfully inherit the shop.

This, while being a member of ROTC, taking flying lessons in a Piper J-3 Cub too, looking ahead to an Army Air Corps future before he was drummed out for insubordination. After being chided during a morning inspection for scuffed shoes and a wrinkled uniform after a long night out, he told the West Point captain to "Sir, go fuck yourself. Sir." This was considered bad form. Insubordinate and unmilitary.

While his father was dubious about "the waste of four years of looking at all those books, studying history, something that already happened," his mother swooned at the sight of him in cap and gown.

As he drops the final pin, the lock opens.

"I'm absentminded and sometimes lose my keys, so this is why I had to learn how to open locks without them," Harry says, finally devising a lame excuse.

"Good try, Harry," Dorothy says.

They walk into the aftermath of a tornado. Holes have been punched in the walls, floorboards lifted and broken. Horsehair from the mattress is spread around like dirty snow, clothing ripped apart, all other possessions smashed.

"Believe it or not, this is an improvement," Harry says.

"I do have to wonder about your British friend," David says, eyebrows raised nearly to his hairline.

"That makes two of us. If he is British," Harry says. "Peter was mixed up in things he didn't tell me about. I had to think the worst when he disappeared, and it looks like I was right."

"His comments regarding gold and your Nazi friend are surely related."

Harry shrugs. "Or it could strictly be politics. Peter has a voice like a foghorn. Just before he was taken away, he was spouting off about Hitler and Salazar, how they're sweethearts. They're sensitive here about their leader."

"Harry's apartment is the Waldorf Astoria compared to this," Dorothy tells her brother, as she looks around and sniffs.

"Have a seat on what's left of Peter's bunk, but be careful of the cockroaches," Harry says, dropping to his knees. "They're so big in this building that they have tattoos."

"I'll stand," the Booths say in unison.

"Let's see how thorough they were on their treasure hunt." Harry flattens on the floor, lifts a floorboard that abuts the hallway, and reaches in as far as he can. "Peter's favorite hiding place and they missed it. Ha!"

He pulls out a bottle of 20-year-old Scotch with something taped to it.

He gives the bottle to Dorothy, brushes his clothing with his hands, and says, "Unwrap the tape, but please don't drop the bottle."

"Calm down, Harry. I wouldn't dream of harming your elixir."

She peels off the paper and tape.

"Oh my good Lord."

She gives David a gold ingot that is half the dimensions of a playing card and three times as thick. Stamped on it is the German eagle inside a wreath. Below the decoration: DEUTSCHE REICHSBANK .999/1000 GOLD and a serial number.

"Gold," David says.

"Gold," Dorothy says.

"Finders keepers," Harry says, snapping his fingers and holding out a hand.

*****

"This validates some of my suspicions regarding your friend," David says, unzipping his briefcase and removing an eight-by-ten photograph. "What I'm about to brief you on takes precedence over any amount of gold."

"A picture does?" Harry says, pocketing the ingot.

"I wasn't prepared to take you into our confidence yet, but this changes things."

"Sure, David. What else have we got to do?"

"Before I show you this photo, Harry, I must warn you, it is disturbing. You may get sick."

Harry cocks a thumb, "Not me. I have a cast-iron constitution, but if you need to hustle to the bathroom, it's down the hall. I gotta warn you, though. You may get sick just going in there."

"Do not take my warning lightly."

Harry waves a hand. "I've seen it all and then some."

Harry takes the photo from David and beholds the corpse of a man who obviously died in agony. His eyes are wide, his face twisted. He could have been in his thirties, forties or fifties. His skin is blotchy and speckled with deep sores.

Harry turns away, holding his mouth, and stumbles out of the room.

"Bathroom's down the hall," David says.

Dorothy goes after Harry and pats his back as he doubles over the toilet. "Take deep breaths. It'll help. I substitute in a health class, you know. Trust my advice."

After Harry composes himself and returns, David says, "We don't know his name, but we are sure he's Jewish. There's a number tattooed on his forearm, see?"

"I'll take your word for it."

"The Nazis do this in their detention camps."

Harry is facing David now, breathing deeply as instructed by Dorothy. He forces himself to look at the photo again.

David says, "Experts believe the poor wretch died of advanced heavy-metal radiation poisoning. An autopsy found the start of four kinds of cancer. He turned up In the Azores, delirious. He'd been a stowaway on a Brazilian freighter that steamed out of here on the Rio Tejo. He was raving about 'Lisbon' and 'mass murder'. Those were the only words anybody could understand before he died. He was flown to London, where the autopsy was done.

"Our ambassador to the Court of St. James, Joseph Kennedy, was informed. Ambassador Kennedy passed along the information to President Roosevelt, who contacted us through Harry Hopkins, one of FDR's closest advisors."

"Whoever *us* is," Harry says. "Is that you and your secret club? Or you and your sis? Or you and your sis and your secret club, plural? When we were kids we had a secret club. Remember? We met in Billy Wiley's tree house. Shouldn't we all have decoder rings like you send away for with cereal box tops?"

David says, "Give it up, Harry, and cease the babbling. I'm not telling you any more than I'm authorized to. The cause of the poisoning is believed to be an enriched radioactive uranium isotope. This is a new scientific offshoot."

"You're talking Greek," Harry says, shaking out a cigarette.

"Please, Harry," Dorothy says.

"Please, Harry. I insist that you refrain from smoking. That makes two vetoes in this confined space," David says.

Harry sticks the smoke back in the pack and says, "First this uranium stuff kills. Next you're gonna say cigarettes kill. And somebody someday will run the four-minute mile and walk on the moon. Oh yeah, and there'll be a radio with pictures in every living room."

Dorothy says, "These advances will happen sooner than your comic book writers think, Harry. Radios with pictures are called televisions."

"No fooling?"

"There was one at the New York World's Fair last year. It had a seven-inch screen."

"Come on. You're making that up."

"If you think televisions belong in one of your spaceship cartoons, Harry, you haven't seen the half of it," David says, taking a newspaper article from his briefcase.

"*The New York Times*," Harry says. "I read it when there's nothing else to read. They sure do like to print bad news."

"Bad news," David says. "This particular edition is an understatement."

Harry sees that it's a headline story in the May 5, 1940 issue: VAST POWER SOURCE IN ATOMIC ENERGY OPENED BY SCIENCE. *Relative of Uranium Found to Yield Force 5 Million Times as Potent as Coal. GERMANY IS SEEKING IT. Scientists Ordered to Devote All time to Research — Tests Made at Columbia.*

"This is the poison that killed that poor guy?"

"One and the same, so it is believed," David says.

Harry uncaps the Scotch, swigs and grimaces. "As smooth as velvet. Good for what ails you."

Dorothy yanks the bottle out of his hand. "That is quite enough."

Harry blows dust and horsehair off the bunk, "I think for a change it'll be smart to sit down to read rather than stand and skim."

CHAPTER 9

As a hard-and-fast rule, Horatio Alger (Harry) Antonelli looks at the pictures before reading an article, especially an article like this with a headline longer than some entire articles. The pictures usually aren't worth a thousand words, but they do tell the erstwhile history major whether or not he wants to read on.

This atomic-energy piece is longer than long and its print is fine. The pictures are of suit-and-tie bookworms in front of big machines, milquetoast guys that he knows have stratospheric IQs. One big thing with dials is called a cyclotron recording machine. Okay, gotta have one of those. In another picture, one of the eggheads is fiddling with complicated tubing. He never saw anything like that in a chem lab, in high school or the UW. Serious business.

"Mad science," Harry says, reading on. "This uranium ore's found everywhere and a pound of it packs as much punch as three million gallons of gasoline after they fiddle with it. A pound of this U-235 stuff, it's got the power of fifteen thousand tons of TNT, three-hundred railroad car loads of it. Hundreds of times of this, thousands of times of that, millions of times of this and that. They're building a bomb that'll make London look like a crater on the moon, huh? How big is a pound of U-235?"

David makes a circle of fingers and thumbs. "Approximately."

"Must be very heavy. Heavier than gold or tungsten?"

"Roughly the same mass."

"Is this uranium hard to get your hands on?"

"Not at all, not in the unrefined ore form," David says. "French Niger and the Belgian Congo in western Africa have plenty in the form of ore called yellowcake."

"I'm not picturing Betty Crocker."

"Yellowcake is not difficult to get to the African coast and ship it up here. Cover the top of the bins with corn or another innocuous product and it's quite easy. Nazi Germany is aggressively pursuing it there. They also have access to ore in Czechoslovakia too, but in much smaller deposits and purity."

"The Nazis are cooking up a bomb like in that article?" Harry says, his mouth dry and sour from this news and from stomach acid and Scotch.

"It is a definite possibility," David says. "If they are, we have to put a halt to it."

"You think here in Lisbon is the obvious place they're doing it, playing with atomic bombs? Good ol' neutral Lisbon?"

David frowns. "Is it in neutral Lisbon or is it that this radiation victim was a misdirection plant? We believe it's the former. That's all we have to go on. The sad soul in the photo had to know that he was doomed, but we surmise that his family was threatened if he didn't cooperate and lie. We could be wrong, though. It could be Madrid or Barcelona or Timbuktu. The Nazis are cunning monsters. They're capable of anything."

Buck Rogers is up against that all the time, Harry thinks, sensibly keeping that thought to himself.

He says, "Okay, why put all your cards here and not in, say, Timbuktu?"

David says, "As I said, the victim is all we have to go on. An educated guess. Because of him, we strongly believe the activity is occurring here in Lisbon."

"So you don't know it to be a fact based on that poor bastard?"

"Not one-hundred percent. But circumstantial evidence tells us it is. Let me pose a hypothetical to you, Harry, an old hand in this city.

Why Lisbon, in your opinion, if it is indeed here?"

Harry thinks for a moment as he adjusts his seating position.

"Well, as we've been saying, Portugal's neutral. If they're whipping up a batch of yellowcake in Germany and the Brits find out, they'd bomb the location to rubble. If they bomb Lisbon, Salazar will be so pissed off, he'll join the Axis. Franco will be right on his heels instead of vice versa."

"A sophisticated view, the same as one major possibility we've arrived at," David says.

"We. There are more of them than you can shake a stick at," Harry says. "And, hey, thanks. Nobody's ever accused me of being sophisticated before."

"You can help us," David says.

"Me?" Harry says.

"We're not in the war yet, but our entry is inevitable. If the Germans are developing a doomsday weapon to use on England or elsewhere, we have to stop them in their tracks," David says. "With Hitler's pathological loathing of Britain, he's not above anything to cripple them. Counterfeiting the English pound, blockading them, killing every last man woman and child, anything."

"So, out with it. Why did you come looking at me, Dave? You have me pegged as a bum."

"Let's just say you aren't realizing your full potential."

"High-class bum, then," Harry says, shrugging.

David Booth almost smiles. "You're a bum who's been here in Lisbon for a period of time, for roughly eight months—"

"How are you finding out this 'roughly' and all else about me? Out with it."

"— in the company of, well, people who aren't upstanding citizens, who may be involved in, shall we say, nefarious activities. You have or can have a finger on things in Lisbon. That's why I'm here, Harry. You're really our only choice. We've been remiss, I'll admit, in getting people on the ground in neutral European countries.

We've been naïve at the highest levels, but don't quote me on that."

"I promise I won't, if you'll tell me who the hell I'd quote you to," Harry says.

That's why Dorothy's here too, the only reason, Harry now knows. It isn't that she can't stand to be away from him. She's bait, pure and simple. Maybe her math and science savvy to help out on the uranium angle too. With him on the hook, her job done, she'll head off to England and jump into bed with her Messerschmitt-killing Spitfire hero.

Harry is getting queasy again. "You're calling me a bum and a crook and asking me to be a spy, a secret agent?"

"If you prefer, we'll deem you our fifth columnist."

"I don't deem. They accused me of that in Madrid, a synonym for public enemy. Another long story."

"Don't worry, Harry. Everything will be on the q.t."

"The last person who told me not to worry is the renter of this flat. Unless I miss my guess, he's at PVDE headquarters being drawn and quartered."

"*Time* and *Life* magazines have been full of stories about fifth columnists here, there and everywhere. It takes a certain *joie de vivre* and keenness for daring that you possess. Have you been reading the magazines?"

"I skim over things. Like the papers, except for the sports page, they're full of rotten news. And it can be too, like when the Rainiers drop a doubleheader."

"Unfortunately, Harry, you're all we have. Portuguese neutrality is such a sham, leaving us far behind the Axis."

"The bottom of the barrel, huh?"

"You said it, not me."

Harry takes a deep breath. "This is a whole bunch to swallow in one mouthful."

"I'm asking you to help save the world."

Harry laughs. "This is too much to swallow in one whole meal."

David doesn't reply.

"Save the world? Wow. Is that all? What's in it for me?"

David balls his fists, the first physical emotion Harry has seen from him since the city basketball championship game against Roosevelt High when a scrappy little guard goaded him into fouling out.

"If this menace isn't stopped and England falls victim to a hideous atomic weapon, she will lose the war, taking all free nations with her. Hitler can take his own sweet time developing weapons to use against us."

Dorothy steps in front of her brother, shielding Harry. "Please work with David. If I hadn't paid your back rent, you'd be on the street. The Portuguese secret police is hunting for you. You tried to drown two of them and a German friend of theirs, and you blew up their car."

"The sights on the Kraut's Luger were off. Is that my fault?"

"Your partner in crime —"

"Peter and I aren't partners and we aren't criminals. Not exactly."

"Oh, please, Harry. You deal in the black market and you smuggle, and perhaps ten other things we don't know about."

"Here we go again. All right, if you want to split hairs. Everybody and his brother is in what you call the black market. It's how things get done in Lisbon. This isn't Seattle, you know. You can't just go to the A&P when you need something. It's the economy, how things work. Since the war started, everything's been crazy."

Dorothy says, "You've told me this before. Econ 101 according to Horatio Alger Antonelli."

David says, "Your partner in crime is missing, probably kidnapped, probably worse. You said so yourself, that German demanded gold from you."

"Gold I know nothing about. Knew nothing about until this. Scout's honor."

"You were thrown out of the Boy Scouts," Dorothy says.

"The Girl Scouts were camped on the other side of the lake. A few of us went on a night hike to test our compasses and look for owls and other nocturnal wildlife, to earn a merit badge. Our compasses were off and it looked like rain, so we—"

David says, "This repartee has been a barrel of laughs, kids, but let's review Portugal's basic economics. Portugal has great quantities of wolframite ore, which Germany doesn't. The ore is smelted into tungsten. It's used for much more than light bulbs. Tungsten is ultra heavy, the same specific gravity as gold, and has the highest melting point of any industrial metal. It's as hard and tough as the dickens, and is used in vital wartime alloys such as hardening machine tools for steel manufacturing. The rest I'm going to tell you is highly classified information."

Harry says, "I can guess, so let me intercept your lecture. It's common knowledge too, but mum's the word. The tungsten ore's shipped to Germany on the sly, so England doesn't find out and get pissed off. Germany ships gold to Swiss banks. Swiss francs go into Portugal's account. Portugal buys gold with the Swiss francs. Lisbon is the last free currency market in Europe. It's hard to keep up with the changing rates and the wheeling and dealing. A bloody fine golden triangle, as my wherever-he-is buddy Peter Owens once put it after a few belts."

David is at a loss for words for a few seconds. "If you know it all, do you have any suggestions where uranium fits in to your golden triangle?"

"Nope, but if it does, it's a golden rectangle that glows in the dark. I don't know, other than money can buy anything, including newfangled uranium bombs."

"The fanatical, insane Nazi agent, this Horst Wessel, demanding gold from you?"

"Jesus Christ, can we finally get off that subject?"

David Booth says. "He can be our bridge, our key."

"Horst and I aren't speaking and he's the type to hold a grudge and

I'm no gumshoe, no secret agent," Harry says. "Anyhow, Horst will eventually find me if I'm unlucky, which I've been lately."

"Gumshoe and secret agent. It's too late for either in the strict definitions of your job title, unfortunately."

"Yes, unfortunately. You're as subtle as a foghorn," Dorothy says.

"I'm also a walking bull's-eye."

David smiles. "As you have intimated, if you don't find trouble, it'll find you."

David's logic is brutally accurate. Harry acquiesces by raising no further objections. He senses a blending of the Sunday funnies and himself, not a comfortable sensation. He's gonna be a superhero without a portfolio.

David's lecture isn't over, but they seldom are, Harry thinks.

Dorothy's eyes are on Harry too. When he's being proctored, he hears, but except for snippets he doesn't listen.

"You'll be doing this for America as much as anyone else. It you don't think that's a worthwhile cause, move to Communist Russia, live in a socialist paradise where there's not enough to eat and somebody pounds on your door in the middle of the night."

Harry looks at the watch he's not wearing.

Dorothy bends, takes him by the chin, raises it, and moves in so closely that he can smell her Ipana. She kisses him lightly on the lips.

"Harry," she whispers.

Harry smiles. "Okay, if I wasn't sold before, I am now."

David says, "All right, Harry, who haven't we covered that you know, who can be used as a starting point?"

"Bartenders, angry landladies, petty hustlers," he says, very deliberately omitting Maria Fernanda.

"Germans besides Herr Wessel?"

"None. Wait. There's a German bookshop in town. I've walked by it. Just the sight of it pisses me off. Hitler this, Hitler that in the windows. It probably has Hitler wallpaper."

"Good idea, Harry," David says.

"Great idea, Harry," Dorothy says. "Expand your nonexistent library and make new friends and enemies."

Harry is warming to the plan. "I'm a history major and I betcha they're peddling distorted history books."

"Outstanding," David says.

He digs a small silvery object out of his briefcase and gives it to Harry.

"What's this?"

"See on the side? A lens. And beside it, a viewfinder. It's a miniature camera."

"A secret camera for secret agents," Harry says.

It fits easily in the palm of his hand. He turns it around and around. Harry is a man who likes toys. "A Minox Riga."

"Yes. Made in Riga, Latvia. Not Germany," David says.

"Good. What and who do I take pictures of?"

"Anything and anybody suspicious."

Harry laughs. "This is Lisbon. I'll need a carload of film."

"I'll trust your discretion. You can bring the exposed film to me whenever we meet."

"You're giving me a tall order. If I nose around and find what you want me to find, then what? I can't tackle these characters by myself. Can you send in the cavalry?"

Dorothy offers Harry a thin smile and says, "If you're not up to it, this has been a wasted trip for us, a terribly wasted trip since there is so little time."

She sure knows how to get his goat, going below the belt. She also knows, or thinks she knows, that she can count on Horatio Alger (Harry) Antonelli when the chips are down. It's extremely unfair of her.

David gives him a short course (short for him) on how to use the camera, showing him where the shutter, viewfinder and settings are. How to load and unload the film.

Saying that it has a stainless steel body and dials that are chrome-plated brass, and can take a lot of abuse, but try not to drop it. The lens is as fast as *f* 3.5, meaning that it's wide-eyed enough for partial darkness. The shutter could be set as fast as 1/1000 of a second, so it can freeze most motion. There's no battery, the user is the battery.

The Minox fits unobtrusively in Harry's shirt pocket like a pack of fags. Harry's no camera bug, but he likes it. All the better if he can needle somebody with the thing. Even wrap his hand around it when he throws a punch; giving his blow some extra oomph, like brass knuckles.

Outside, as Dorothy steps into the street and waves at a taxi, David steps in front of Harry and says, "My sister is much too good for you, Antonelli."

"I know she is. That's old news. What does it have to do with the price of eggs?"

David points a finger at Harry as he walks around him, toward the taxi Dorothy has flagged down.

"We're here only because your country needs you."

"Speaking of old news."

"They may end up teaching history you helped change," David says.

"Yeah?"

"But before you get a swelled head, if you accomplish this, it will be classified for ages. We'll all be long gone before the files are released to the public."

Shit. No fame, no fortune.

"Hey, Dave, before you go away, do secret agents get paid? Turn my pockets inside out and all you'll see is lint."

David nods at Dorothy's large purse. She comes to them, removes a wad of escudos, and gives the money to Harry.

"Wonder Woman, you're the spy ring's treasurer?"

She sticks her tongue out at him and returns to the taxi.

David says, "You are not on anybody's payroll as an employee. There is no set salary, no employer, no contract."

"That's hunky-dory with me. I hate paperwork."

"Any further comments or questions?"

Harry shakes his head as he counts the escudos. Not Rockefeller great, but not bad. He can eat and drink on it and pay for a cheap room, but it isn't enough to bribe anybody. This is his first salaried job since part-time work in college. It might be his last if he doesn't watch his p's and q's.

He'll do whatever he can. And do whatever it is as he tries not to be killed by everyone with an axe to grind, a growing number.

Harry watches the cab pull away.

Sometimes he hates himself for doing the right thing, and this is one of those times.

CHAPTER 10

R eality is sinking in. Like a lead sinker.

It's damn unfair of the Booths and their spymasters to expect me to do what Buck Rogers and Flash Gordon and the Phantom do routinely every Sunday, Harry thinks, moping and brooding, on his way to the bookshop. The writers and cartoonists can have the good guys do the job with the stroke of a pen. Being the savior of mankind—not so easy in real life.

Maybe Harry likes the comics too much, just slightly too much, but he can't jump into the pages and save humanity. Can't be done. David bringing Dorothy along as a siren to entice him, that's doubly unfair. Comparing him to her Spitfire flyboy, Harry has already been chalked up as a sissy with much to prove.

But if he can pull it off...

Harry's mission in general—as specific as it can be, thanks to limited information—is to poke his head into a hornet's nest, à la *Kristallnacht*. Multiple hornet's nests.

With all due respect to the poor people terrorized then, there's a helluva lot more at stake on this uranium deal.

He has to come up with a plan how to locate the uranium factory— if there is such a thing—without dying for his country or anybody else's. He isn't palsy-walsy with any Nazi, and Peter Owen is missing, unable to steer him in the right and/or wrong direction, even if he could or would. So the Nazi bookshop it has to be.

Harry is thinking about this and things less relevant as he trudges on. Such as the similarities and differences between Seattle and Lisbon. Seattle's 1940 census is 368,000, Lisbon's double that. Both towns are bumpy and on water.

Lisbon's built lower to the ground than U.S. cities: their cathedrals are their skyscrapers. Seattle has the 42-floor, 500-feet-tall Smith Tower. When built in 1914, it was the tallest building west of the Mississippi. At 27 stories, the Northern Life Tower is no midget either.

Seattleites worry that they'll be overrun by the Japs if the U.S. enters the war. For *lisboetas*, it's the Nazis. Different fascists, same anxieties.

In the Chiado shopping district where the bookshop is, goods rationed or nonexistent in Nazi Europe or heavily-rationed-Britain are on market shelves and street displays. Basic foodstuffs like rice and tinned meat that are readily available to Portuguese and ho-hum in the States are European luxuries.

Seattle's business and shopping district has it over Lisbon's hands-down, jam-packed with anything anybody could possibly want or need. Nearby movie theatres show the latest Hollywood films, none of them politically censored.

Harry comes upon the corner taken up by the German bookstore. It's at Rua Garrette and Rua Novo do Carmo, a substantial building with ALEMANHA plastered on one side, DEUTSCHLAND on the other. It's probably a popular stop for *lisboetas* who swallow the Kraut pitch that they're the only thing standing between Portugal and godless Communism.

Harry walks into a cornucopia of propaganda. You can't get past *Mein Kampf* or the many photos of Hitler, some wallet-sized, some framed, some protected in cellophane. The *Mein Kampfs* are stacked like cordwood. Be it a Nuremberg rally or a small bookshop, these birds know how to put on a show.

Adolf is all over the walls. There's the *Führer* in a brown shirt, in the formative years of the Nazi Party. And there in leather shorts and suspenders, lederhosen at its most stylish, wild, greasy hair in all of them. That toothbrush mustache and those wild bug eyes too.

How Horst Wessel and all the German knuckleheads regard Hitler as their messiah is beyond him. The guy badly needs a Hollywood make-up artist and hair stylist. Plastic surgery, of course. Wardrobe help too. Harry's no clotheshorse, but Hitler's a fucking joke. As a matinee idol, he's a whole bunch closer to The Three Stooges than Tyrone Power.

Harry browses. If you're tired of *der Führer*, there are caricatures of Jews aplenty, crudely simian, alone and being abused by Nazi supermen. Disgusting.

Speaking of Nuremberg, on the wall above the counter, there Adolf is, a poster-sized shot, thousands and thousands of troops frozen in formation focused on one man alone. Harry wonders what you'd do if you'd been standing for hours and have to take a leak.

Harry's the shop's only customer. He points at the poster and asks the clerk that question. It goes unanswered.

"If you gotta go, you gotta go, so if you raise your hand and ask to go potty, do they say okay or do they shoot you on the spot?"

The clerk has been dusting a book display and just looks at him. There's an instantaneous dislike between him and Harry, which Harry likes.

"You don't speak English, huh? I think that was a fair question. College graduation was similar for me, sitting and standing for a long time, but the speeches were by ordinary windbags, telling us the world's our oyster, not some fucking homicidal madman."

Harry studies the picture again, thoughtfully, stroking his chin, as if in an art gallery.

"I don't see any outhouses anywhere in that crowd. Do you?"

"I do speak English and comprehend your every word."

The clerk is pear-shaped, thirtyish and beady-eyed, soft and pasty. Round glasses rim eyes as cold as a wagon load of ice.

He has shaved sidewalls and short hair on top of the whitish blonde of Hollywood's platinum blondes. On him, it isn't flattering. Harry's barber in Seattle charges two-bits. If this bookshop clerk pays that much, it's highway robbery.

He really does look familiar.

A plaque on the counter by the cash register identifies him as DIETER.

"You *sprecken* zee English good, Hans Dieter. Did you really catch every word I said?"

"Yes," he says flatly.

"You really know your onions, Dieter Fritz. You've got *Mein Kampf* in English too, I see."

"We are honored to carry it in five languages. German, French, English, Spanish and Portuguese."

"That's swell. Did I hear your heels click, Hans?" Harry says, picking up a *Mein Kampf* and paging through it, reading aloud at passages that stop him in his tracks. "'It is not truth that matters, but victory. Who says I am not under the special protection of God? The very first essential for success is a perpetually constant and regular employment of violence. If you want to shine like the sun, first you must burn like it. To conquer a nation, first disarm its citizens.' I could go on and on, but you probably have this piece of shit memorized. Your boss man, Hans Fritz Dieter, he's daffier than Daffy Fucking Duck. He's got bats in the belfry. He's as mean as a fucking snake too. Back where I come from, he'd be committed to where the jackets have those sleeves so your arms can't move, not even to wipe away the drool."

Harry can see the clerk's neck veins now.

"Well, I apologize. Could be I'm being too hard on Adolf. Might be his problems upstairs are due to the syph. Caught a dose when he was younger. Those little worms now, they've come home to roost, boring tunnels in his brain. They say that's happening to Al Capone, another mean, fucking mad-dog crook."

Harry tosses the *Mein Kampf* carelessly back on the stack. "I see you have Benito Mussolini's life story too. The guy's a joke, you know. He made the trains run on time, so what? They don't run anywhere important. His army can't fight their way out of a paper bag and the last time anything important happened in Rome was when Caligula's Praetorian Guard hacked him into mincemeat."

Harry knows he's rambling, disjointed. He doesn't care; he's having too much fun. He's fulfilling his secret mission the only way he knows how.

"My mother sends me books when she knows where to send them, bad son that I am," Harry says. "She belongs to the Book of the Month Club."

Dieter says nothing.

"*Mein Kampf* isn't available through them, huh?"

More silence.

"By sending me books, she shames me into keeping in touch with her and Dad. As I said, I'm not a good son. Do you have a mother and father, Fritz?"

He doesn't answer.

"One of my favorites came to me while I was in Prague. It's *The Big Sleep* written by some guy named Raymond Chandler. He has a detective character named Philip Marlowe. The detective gets to the bottom of things by investigating people and places you wouldn't normally want to go, but you have to in order to solve the crime. Marlowe can be rude too if that's what it takes. Do you understand what I'm saying, Hans Fritzendieter? Anything you have to do to get the bad guy and give him what he deserves."

Harry sniffs and lifts a foot. "There's a great bookshop in downtown Seattle. Shorey's on Third Avenue. It's huge and smells terrific, like paper old and new."

Harry looks at the bottom of his shoe, sniffs again, and wrinkles his nose. "Not like here, which smells like something you step in."

Dieter doesn't answer.

"Cat got your tongue, Fritz?" Harry points at a wall, making a pistol out of his fingers. "All these pictures of Hitler you have ready for framing, they must be popular items. I look at him and I think of Ming the Merciless, except that Adolf isn't Oriental. Same evil eyes, though. Know who Ming is?"

Harry keeps his eyes on him for a reaction but receives none.

"He rules the planet Mongo with an iron fist, just like your hero would like to do on this planet. In the evil department, I'd have to say, Ming is small potatoes compared to 'Dolf."

"What? Do? You? Want?"

"I'm looking at these pictures of him, which I sure don't want. They're like pin-ups, you know. We have Betty Grable, you have your *Führer*. Boy, I'm glad I'm a red-blooded American, not German."

Harry smiles. "I'm curious. Do you beat your meat looking at Adolf. Me, I gotta say I prefer Betty."

"You are a Jew?"

"Jesus Christ, here we go again. Is that a question or an answer?"

"You tell me."

The clerk is reddening, so Harry goes for a double-header. "A Communist too and proud of it, Hans. I visit Russia every chance I get."

Harry twirls a finger at a picture of a younger Hitler, leading his storm troopers. "I can see him in a bathing suit, like Grable, him and some little boys."

"Get out of my store, Jew! I do not permit Jews in this store. Do you not read newspapers? Do you not know of the Third Reich? We are sweeping through Europe. When the *Führer* rules the world you and your kind will no longer exist."

Harry sweeps a hand. "You Nazis love book burnings, don't you? Anything you think is a threat, you light a match to it. All this smelly garbage in here, if you ask me, you oughta toss gasoline to it and set it on fire. Get rid of the dogshit aroma."

"Are you threatening arson?"

"Don't tempt me."

"Out!"

"Okay, Hans, you're hurting my feelings, but I can take a hint."

At the door, Harry says, "Say limburger, Fritz."

He snaps the catatonic Dieter's picture with the Minox and says, "Oh yeah. Have a nice day."

TRIVIAL NOTE: "Have a nice day," that insincere and meaningless neologism, did not become common usage until decades later. Nor did "poster boy" and "political correctness," characteristics that Harry nonetheless lacks.

Outside, he sees the crazed Nazi on the phone, red-faced and yelling, eyes locked on Harry.

It comes to him. Dieter resembles Heinrich Himmler, a failed chicken farmer who's now killing far more people than he ever did birds. Bookshop Dieter could be his albino kid brother.

Harry affords him the same middle-digit Nazi salute that had gotten him into a pickle at *Kristallnacht* and walks off.

Thinking: One hornet's nest is a'buzzing, a metaphorical bonfire a'burning.

Now he's cooking with gas, eligible for a pat on the head from David. And if he's luckier than lucky, a pat from Dorothy somewhere else.

If he isn't the Nazi Party's Fifth Columnist Public Enemy Number One in this town, he doesn't know who the hell is.

CHAPTER 11

Café A Brasileira is two blocks up the hill from the Nazi bookshop. It's a Lisbon landmark, around before Harry was born. The interior is polished brass, tile, decorative lamps, laid out like an old-timey saloon. The Brasileira caters to high-brainpower drinkers like writers and intellectuals. Harry isn't sure if most writers qualify as brainy, but they are big drinkers, he'll give them that.

He sits outside at a table, under an umbrella, with a view of one side of the bookshop and the corner. It isn't the side with the door, but it'll have to do. Everybody who glances at him makes him wish he had a beret he can ride low, covering part of his public-enemy face. A notebook too, knocking out the next great novel.

Even the cute ladies giving him the evil eye (he thinks), there could be a Wonder Woman–type of Nazi among them. Get one in the right mood so she's wearing nothing but a sneer, a swastika armband, a whip, and—

Sipping beer, he fiddles with the Minox, cupping it, holding it to an eye, wondering if it has telephoto range.

He keeps a steady watch on what he can see of the Nazi bookstore, hoping that Dieter, the Himmler-esque storekeeper, will leave to report the impertinent American Communist Jew or at least get through on the phone to the local fascists, Wessel or whoever, anyone who brings in the Nazi cavalry, anyone who'll lead him to the next step in the chain. No such thing in his field of vision occurs.

Dieter, the creepy little sissy, is probably too busy anyway. He's by himself and customers are dribbling in. Some look sheepish, like they're entering a dirty bookstore, which they are.

Harry gives up after a couple of hours, figuring he'll slip back just before late-afternoon closing time and follow creepy little Dieter. In an odd way, Harry's feelings are hurt because he isn't being taken seriously as an expert spy. A boozer and loafer and an allegedly-Jewish troublemaker, yep; a secret agent nope. Creepy little disrespectful Dieter.

Harry hasn't the foggiest notion what to do next, a sweeping metaphor for his time in Europe. It's like waiting for next Sunday's funnies to see how Buck and Flash and the rest escape their cliff-hanging quandaries and move forward to thwart the enemy and get into their next jam.

It boils down to saving the world right now or having another drink. He can only do what he can do when he can do it.

In order to quench his thirst in a proper atmosphere, though, Harry takes a taxi to the Canção. He can easily walk the kilometer-and-a-half, but he has secret-agent wages in his pocket and there's no use asking for problems above and beyond what he already has.

His paranoia in full bloom, he imagines bull's-eyes, one on his back, another on his forehead, another over his family jewels. Harry Antonelli, human pincushion.

During the harum-scarum ride, he daydreams to shunt his mind from sudden automotive death, the tin can of a cab missing a high-speed turn and hurtling through a shop window. He pictures himself in the Sunday funnies. His own strip or as a guest star in "Wonder Woman", collaborating with her on saving the world. And later, her showing her gratitude in panels that cannot be shown to a family readership. A super power here and there wouldn't hurt either.

But in real life, all he has at his disposal are his fists and his wits.

Harry walks into the Canção, hardly able to believe his eyes. Sitting at the darkest table in a rear corner are Peter Owen and

Maria Fernanda Ramos. Sitting closely, no space between them, holding hands, poised in mid-kiss.

They quickly slide apart at the sight of him.

Horatio Alger (Harry) Antonelli, commissioned to save the planet, cannot even keep his pathetic personal life from coming to pieces.

Dazed, befuddled, and stupefied, he about-faces and is barely out the door when Peter has him by an arm.

"Harry, laddie, easy, it's not what you think."

Harry turns, jerking away his hand. "Are you saying I'm seeing things?"

"She was comforting me. It has been an untidy time for this lad. These dusky little Portuguese lasses are highly emotional. I told my terrifying story and she was comforting me, no more."

"Tell me this terrifying story of yours."

Harry listens to his spiel, delivered in a touch of a New England twang, then sailing across the Atlantic to Ireland and England, his patoises of the day. Peter claims that he had been rudely escorted to PVDE headquarters by the bully boys in this pub and given the third degree about a number of topics he had absolutely no knowledge of.

The secret police demanded to know about gold, and smuggling of commodities and, for a nice price, refugees. Since he is a party to nothing illegal, is innocent of all accusations, and cannot confess to anything he does not know, he was eventually released. Considerately, since Harry is his dearest friend, he spares him the painful details of the, ahem, interviews.

It's a fishy story, a whole wharf's worth of fishy, Harry believes. Fishy at low tide.

"That's rich, Peter."

"What are you saying, Harry?" Peter says, eyes wide and innocent.

The PVDE takes nobody's word for anything, but to challenge Peter further is pointless.

"You and Maria Fernanda?"

"She was consoling me. I am bruised and contused in areas you cannot see. The PVDE learned their trade from the Gestapo, you know, and have become masters at it. Harry, that comely little lass, she is devoted to you."

"Applesauce, she is. I was worried sick when the PVDE hauled you away. What else were they after, what did they think you know that you haven't told me about?"

"Oh, nothing in particular, hoping to hit a jackpot on every crime since Guy Fawkes and his gunpowder. I believe it was routine harassment of foreign nationals with entrepreneurial interests. If I hadn't repeatedly informed them that I was a citizen of the Crown, I'd still be there."

"Where are our corks and Maria Fernanda's Citroën?"

"Our goods were confiscated. For further investigation." Peter sighs theatrically. "I am trying to be philosophical. Civil servants everywhere are underpaid."

"Our shipping connection, João?"

"The slippery rotter is in the PVDE's employ. As you Yanks say, he's a stool pigeon. A freelance swine for sale to the premium bidder. Just like us, frankly, and half the people in Lisbon in these turbulent times, so who are we to cast stones? That's how the secret police got on to us and snatched me up. I have no doubt João, the shifty bloke, received a share of what is rightfully ours for being a tipster."

"And here I thought it was routine harassment."

"Lines blur in this town, Harry. You know this. Nothing *and* everything are as they seem."

"I give up trying to make any sense out of this, Peter. Again, Maria Fernanda's Citroën?"

"In police impoundment. They have it in a yard by the docks. I was wishing her well in her effort to have it released, giving her courage."

Harry looks around and behind Peter. Maria Fernanda is gone, unavailable to be consoled by Harry. Convenient.

He walks to the bar and asks for a whiskey. Peter tags along, asking for the same, laying down escudos for their drinks.

Harry ignores Peter's free-floating chatter as he sips and thinks, recollecting how they met. Dates and times blur, but it was when he lived in the Alfama dump before his present Alfama dump. That dump didn't have a chain-smoking, port-guzzling landlady, but the accommodations were comparable.

It was on a rainy afternoon in a riverfront dive west of Praça de Comércio, on the way to Belém, two losers sitting at the bar, keeping dry, chewing the fat. They had big ideas, ideas that grew bigger as the afternoon progressed.

With Peter's contact and a trucker acquaintance of Harry's from Porto, they collaborated to export a quantity of port wine, nary a bottle younger than 20 years. They did so without troubling overworked tax and customs officials, and made a tidy profit.

To celebrate, Peter brought Harry here, to the Café do Canção.

"You'll love the *fado* singer, Harry," Peter had said. "She has the voice of an angel."

And so she did and so he had.

Harry polishes off the whiskey, wondering how you say "play Cupid" in British English.

"Peter, gold."

"Gold?"

"Gold. You first brought up the subject and it's not far from your mind."

"Gold, yes. You know, that mesmerizing yellow metal. Gold has driven men mad since the beginning of time."

"Have you been to your flat lately?"

"Why do you ask?"

"Oh, just flapping my gums."

Peter says with a straight face, "No, I haven't returned to it. If the PVDE decides to have an encore with me, that's the first spot they'd look, don't you suppose? Why do you ask, Harry?"

Harry shrugs and looks at the poster of Prime Minister Salazar, who is looking disapprovingly at him.

"As we have often discussed, as half the *lisboetas* have discussed. In Portugal's context. Gold, tungsten, Swiss francs. What brought this on?"

Harry summarizes his misadventure with the PVDE and the Nazi, editing out the Booths, his secret mission to save the world, and Peter's gold ingot in his pocket, which may be either a nest egg or a time bomb.

Peter laughs heartily and orders another round. "You have had a time of it too, lad. This town will never bore you."

"Uranium."

"Word association, is it? That is a new one on me. An exotic and heavy mineral, is it not?"

"It is," Harry says.

"Uranium in what context? I recall it from school textbooks."

"Strictly from way back when?"

"Those were the days."

"In no other context?"

"Is it associated with an animal, vegetable or mineral? You can be confounding."

"Never mind," Harry says.

"There are times, Harry, when you are as mysterious and inscrutable as any Oriental."

Harry laughs. "I'm mysterious and inscrutable?"

"You've been altogether too serious and coy, mate. Whatever's bothering you, I am with you, through thick and thin."

"Thanks. I need to visit the WC as you Brits call it."

Harry walks down the hall and out the back door.

He's going to do whatever he's going to do on his own.

CHAPTER 12

On a vividly sunny afternoon at Berchtesgaden in the German Alps.

Eva Braun suns herself in the nude outside the chalet, behaving like a common street prostitute, driving him crazy when she does that. Hitler has locked himself in the bathroom.

Propped against the sink is a drawing done by his favorite artist, who had done many of him in heroic poses, drawings framed and shown in places of honor throughout the Third Reich, on fireplace mantles, and in meeting halls and churches. Everywhere. Or else.

The artist had done sketches for him of a nude Eva too, her legs spread, displaying the filth between them. The sketches have little effect on him, aside from disgust.

EDITORIAL NOTE: Hitler really should lighten up on her. Eva stuck with him until the very end in the Führerbunker when most of his upper echelon set their sights on Argentina and Paraguay. On 4/29/1945, they tied the knot in a small civil ceremony (when he popped the question is unknown). Their honeymoon was quite short in both time and extent of travel. On April 30, she bit down on a cyanide capsule while, with a pistol (a Luger?), he blew out what remained of his brains.

Nevertheless, Hitler focuses on the drawing. It's infinitely more erotic than Eva sunning herself.

The artist has incorporated the photographs Hitler had taken from

Lisbon, the prints of the Radium Girls with the worst poisoning, with one of Winston Churchill. The drawing is a masterpiece. Churchill's fat face is emaciated, jaw receding in advanced necrosis, nose bleeding, face covered with pustulating sores, his crotch eaten away as if by worms. He is in excruciating pain.

It is now Hitler's second favorite piece of art, trailing only the one done of him standing on a platform at a meeting, enlightening the very first National Socialists. It was 1920 and the widely-distributed print was entitled *In the Beginning was the Word*.

Mesmerized by the agonized Churchill and masturbating furiously, he ejaculates. Dizzy from the exertion, gasping, seeing spots, the *Führer* grabs the counter before he loses his balance and falls against the toilet.

As he wipes semen from his hand and penis, Hitler feels no letdown, no guilt as he now and then does with Eva on the rare occasion when he is able to perform, and only after she squats, a foot on each side of his prone abdomen and defecates. Often there is a second arousal after she spanks him vigorously, repeatedly shrieking *Juden*.

Otherwise, Adolf Hitler is incapable of guilt.

His thoughts turn to that radioactive powder that will torture Winston Churchill to death for real and millions of Londoners too. A photograph of an agonized Churchill will produce an orgasm like no other.

The scientists had promised "weeks at most" before it was ready to use on London. Adolf Hitler is an impatient man. The old saying, *Rome wasn't destroyed in a day*, does not apply. 'Weeks at most' is too long, he decides. The lightning-fast blitzkrieg came to pass because of his genius and his alone. It must continue is every aspect and form.

The *Führer* pulls up his trousers, adjusting the organs within, his one and only testicle (a secret) and a *circumcised* penis (a State secret!). And since he will be burned to a crisp outside the Führerbunker five years later, after his and Eva's suicides, what nobody including himself can know without an autopsy is that Adolf Hitler has an ovary. He isn't hermaphroditic, but the ovary makes possible a mesmerizing soprano pitch at the height of his frenetic speeches to the masses, without loss of volume or psychological force. This ability isn't, as he believes, a gift from God, but the effect of a recessive gene.

Hitler cinches his belt, thinking of the Lisbon operation. This deadly-radiation project was Reinhard Heydrich's bright idea, his and Himmler's. Hitler loves the sobriquets bestowed upon Reinhard by his enemies: The Hangman, the Butcher of Prague, the Blonde Beast, and Heydrich and Himmler together, the Dark Twins.

To Hitler they are all badges of honor. Reinhard Heydrich is totally, unquestioningly obedient and he knows how to crack the whip. He is impatient to liquidate each and every subhuman on Earth, as quickly and efficiently as possible, a man after his own heart.

Next order of business, after a final underwear adjustment, is to pick up the telephone and order Reinhard immediately to Lisbon to change the weeks-at-most promise to a days-at-most ultimatum.

And too, have him look into a report by Portuguese intelligence operatives passed along to the Gestapo that American agents in Lisbon have developed a secret ray machine that renders one invisible. The Portuguese are an inferior race and their PVDE has much to learn, so Hitler takes the report with a grain of salt. But Reinhard can follow up on it while there. Anything, too, he can learn of Lisbon locals harboring refugee Jews will be a bonus.

Hitler checks himself in the mirror. He dabs off remaining perspiration and slicks down his hair.

That magical uranium powder, he thinks, smiling at himself.

Eight million dead Londoners. It will be like an early Christmas present.

CHAPTER 13

Rocco Antonelli walks in the front door after work to see his wife Joanne holding a postcard, smiling from ear to ear like it's Christmas morning.

He takes it from her and sits in his easy chair. They live in south Seattle in a tidy neighborhood where everybody knows everybody else, which in his opinion can be good or bad. It's a one-story home with a weedless lawn and siding that Rocco faithfully repaints every three years. It has a full basement where the boys had their rooms.

Out the window across the street at the end of the block, he can see the Booth home. Of similar architecture, it's twice the size of theirs. A nice man, Dr. Booth doesn't lord it over anyone.

"I'll wager a week's income it's not from Harry."

Joanne Antonelli's smile fades. "You win."

It's a picture postcard airmailed from Dorothy Booth, an overhead shot of New York City, showing the skyscrapers, the Empire State Building and the Chrysler Building. It looks to Rocco like their tip-tops shoot up into outer space.

"All she says is to wish her bon voyage," Rocco says. "Going to Europe, I hope she steers clear of those Nazi U-boats they have out there. David, that snooty brother of hers, should be tagging along, chaperoning her."

"I wish they were taking that fancy flying boat."

"A ticket on that contraption? For that much dough, you can buy a brand-new car," Rocco says. "Not a Cadillac or Packard, but a nice

107

car. A Ford or a Plymouth. Her dad may be a dentist, but he's not made of money."

"Dorothy never mentions David. If I ask how and what he's doing, she clams up."

"He's a secret G-man, is what I think," Rocco Antonelli says, nodding. "As far as I'm concerned, that boy's too smart for his own good. Always has been."

"Well, I'm praying for Dorothy. Him too if he's with her," Joanne Antonelli says, taking the postcard back, which she rests on the fireplace mantle, a place of honor. "She's going just for the summer to England."

"We can hope she gets back before all hell breaks loose over there. A fine young lady, that Dorothy, she'll be steering clear of Harry if she knows what's good for her," Rocco says, who doesn't pray about anything.

"I lost my brother Fred in the Great War, you know," Joanne says. "Harry and Dorothy and everybody, they need to get out and stay out of Europe. It's a powder keg and always will be. Those Germans and that crazy Hitler of theirs, they follow him like sheep."

Rocco steps out of his coveralls. "She'll be sailing home at the end of the summer just in the nick of time, like Harry said he'd do way back in '38. With that war of theirs, everything's blowing up sky-high over there."

Rocco's Body and Fender on Empire Way, half a mile from home, is a three-stall shop: just Lou, their other son, another body man, and a painter. Rocco can't sit in the office in a coat and tie like some big executive swell. He works on the line when there's a lot to do and there aren't any visitors pestering him.

It's a comfort to Rocco that Lou has no highfalutin ideas in his head. Lou's a year younger than Harry and a century more mature. He's on his own, living in a boarding house, saving up for a ring so he can pop the question to Julia, a really sweet little gal he's been going steady with since the eighth grade. She does typing and steno for a big insurance company downtown, bringing in a little money too. The shop will be in good hands when it's time for Rocco to call it quits and Joanne will get the grandchildren she's so eager for.

Joanne takes the coveralls from him. "The last we heard from Harry, you know, he was in Lisbon, Portugal, doing Heaven knows what."

"Heaven knows what, that's about the size of it," Rocco says sourly.

Joanne keeps a tidy single-story house, plus the basement where the boys had their rooms. She has doilies and trifles in the living room, everything just so. She looks at a silver-framed Harry on the mantle in his college football uniform, a snarling smile inside his leather helmet as he clutches a football with both hands.

Rocco likes football, but doesn't understand why his son wanted to get the daylights knocked out of him every autumn Saturday. That didn't stop Rocco and Joanne from attending at least half the home games and listening to the others and to all the road games on the radio. On the edges of their seats.

He never understood the boy at all. In the back of his mind, he thought that it all started with Joanne putting her foot down that he be called Horatio Alger instead of a good Italian name like Carmine or Silvio. She said she'd carried him around for nine months, the last three in the heat of the summer, so she ought to have the final word.

He couldn't argue with that.

After he bathes, Rocco sits in the living room while Joanne finishes fixing dinner. He's poured himself a generous glassful of dago red from a laundry bleach bottle with a ring handle. He'd begun making wine during Prohibition, and is known throughout the area as the best vintner around.

After the Powers That Be came to their senses and repealed the stupid Volstead Act that handed the country over to gangsters, Rocco saw no reason to stop. His red is as good as any the grocery store crooks want an arm and a leg for. Add a quart bottle of it to a bag of flour and a dozen eggs, and you're out two bucks.

Rocco has the Philco console on, Benny Goodman turned down low. That goddamn cat of Harry's is sitting in a corner by a lamp, staring at him. It's like an African voodoo stare.

The goddamn thing's perched on a chair that's been passed down on Joanne's side of the family since Christ was a corporal. High-backed with old-timey cloth, they saw some just like it in *Gone with the Wind*, which Joanne dragged him downtown to see last year. No one's permitted to sit in the antique chair except guests and that goddamned cat. It's like she's substituted the thing for Harry.

Rocco and the cat have a mutual hatred, worsened by the fact that Rocco can't lift a finger against it, and the goddamn cat knows he can't. How he'd love to take it for a one-way ride into the woods where it can attack wolves and bears instead of neighborhood cats and dogs. Rocco is goddamn sick and tired of apologizing and paying vet bills.

When Harry was a kid, Rocco had wondered about him and cats, but he came to realize that there wasn't anything wrong with the boy after all. Not in that regard.

He saw his son carry two would-be tacklers into the end zone in a game against Oregon State. He'd seen helmets go flying, Harry's and the guys' he'd hit. They were in the stands when a star UCLA halfback had to be taken off in a stretcher, thanks to Harry's open-field tackle that lifted him off his feet and planted him on the ground flatter than a pancake.

There was one thing (among many) that had Rocco scratching his head about the boy. When Harry was a squirt, he'd paid a day's income for circus tickets, front-row seats. The kid loved it, the elephants, the fire eater, the nut case shot out of a cannon, everything. Then a couple of clowns on unicycles came by so close you could touch them. Maybe it was the booze on their breath or the paint on their faces, downturning their lips like they were frowning, that made

Harry hysterical. Rocco didn't know, but he had to take Harry out of there. They never talked about it, then or since.

The goddamn cat keeps staring. A stray that showed up eight or nine years ago, it has a whole lot of Harry in him and vice versa. If trouble doesn't come to them, they'll go out looking for it.

Tabby tires of the staring contest, yawns, and begins licking its privates. Rocco mutters a curse and drinks his wine, thinking again of Harry wasting four years of book learning at the University of Washington, studying history, something that'd already happened.

The boy should've taken a cue from Chuck Shimizu, his best chum, who's going to be a doctor and make some real dough. Harry and Chuck were high school track stars, about all they have in common. The Shimizus, all of them, are nice folks. Not everyone thinks so; just because the Japs over there in Japan are sneaky bastards itching for a fight.

Rocco gets up, studies the postcard, and yells into the kitchen. "Dorothy's too good for him."

"You and I know that," Joanne yells back. "If Dorothy could only corral him for good and lead him to the altar, she could change him. I gave her a book to give to him if they happen to run into each other."

Rocco laughs and says, "Give it up, kiddo."

"You pooh-pooh me, but I know she can straighten him out if she has half a chance."

Rocco smiles and drinks his wine. He says nothing; no point to. He thinks of Harry, thinking that he's too dreamy for his own good. He'd spend half of every Sunday reading and rereading the funny papers. Spending the day in outer space with Buck Rogers.

Rocco Antonelli hadn't gone far in school, but he knows that all women believe they can change their men, but none of them ever do.

Why even try?

Why the hell hook up with someone in the first place if he needs changing?

Rocco finishes his glass. If he was a praying man, he'd say one for

Harry, that he'll keep his nose out of trouble. The boy goes through life like he played football, lowering his head and smashing his way through.

Europe, the way it is with that crazy Hitler and his tanks and airplanes, whatever the boy is up to, he may be biting off a helluva lot more than he can chew.

CHAPTER 14

Horatio Alger (Harry) Antonelli's thought process has been aided by the hootch at the Canção.

Herewith his convoluted, illogical logic: A hunted man who returns to his home is a low-grade moron. Harry is many things, but not a low-grade moron. Ergo, his growing list of enemies know this, so they know he will not under any circumstances return to his home.

Besides, why isn't he hearing hoofbeats, like a Tom Mix or Red Ryder posse? Can it be they're keeping their distance, waiting to see where he'll go next, what he'll do? Something to keep in mind.

Harry is thinking all this as he chins himself up to the balconies and into his flat.

Nightfall is coming soon. His plan is to change clothes, then get back to the German bookstore and see where Baby Albino Himmler goes after he shuts down for the day. The Nazi sissy definitely is a weak spot, a starting point.

As he unbuttons his shirt, there's a knock on the door.

Harry opens the door a crack, looking for unwelcome visitors, his usual kind.

Dorothy Booth pushes the door in his face and makes a production out of sniffing. "For Heaven's sake, Antonelli, you smell like a distillery. If I were the storm troopers, I'd be knocking on your door with a sledgehammer."

"I'm being careful."

She laughs and hands him a book. "Harry Antonelli being careful?"

"Don't scoff. It's possible."

"I'd forgotten about it until I unpacked. *For Whom the Bell Tolls*, by Ernest Hemingway. It's set in the Spanish Civil War and it's said to be very good. Your mother gave it to me when I last saw her. She didn't know I was going to see you in Europe, but mothers instinctively know things. Harry, what's wrong?"

She might as well have slapped his face with that book.

He wipes his eyes, trying to hide the waterworks. "I am the world's shittiest son, bar none."

She hugs him. "There is time for you to reform, you know. You're not a hundred years old."

"How about I reform at the age of ninety-nine?"

"If you survive this mission, you won't survive the reckless daredevil in you. There isn't a snowball's chance in hell you'll make it halfway to age ninety-nine."

A downstairs door slams.

Harry looks out the window and sees two unfamiliar sedans. Buicks, he thinks.

"Rude bastards. The assholes won't leave me alone. Let's vamoose out of here."

"Harry, how did they know?"

"They're not obeying logic is how."

"What?"

"I'll explain as soon as I can explain it to myself."

They run up the stairs to the fourth floor and outside, and climb rickety iron stairs onto the roof. Pigeons flutter away from steeply-sloping red tile. As Harry holds her hand, they lean inward and make their way to the edge where he's laid a ladder. He has stored it by the gutter for this very purpose, to escape from his building to the roof of the one across the back street.

"No," Dorothy says, hands clamped on a ladder rung.

"Don't look down," Harry advises. "Make believe it's only a foot off the ground."

"I can't do this. I cannot."

"Come on. It's only ten feet."

"It's the Grand Canyon, a mile down."

"Okay, fifteen or twenty or thirty or forty feet, not an inch more."

Midway across the ladder, Harry turns and reaches out a hand for her, backing as he helps her across one slow rung at a time. The neighboring roof has ridges and is flat. Harry lays the ladder on the roof and takes Dorothy to a chimney. On the other side of it, out of view, they sit on old sofa cushions.

"Just us and the pigeons, and they've taken the hint."

"You've done this before," Dorothy says, raising up and looking for unpleasant substances.

"Everybody should have an escape plan. Once in a while, I pull one out of my ass, er, a hat."

"How old were you when your father first paddled your butt for cussing?"

"Nine or ten."

"When your mother washed your mouth out with Ivory when she caught you?"

"A little older, and it was Camay. She'd buy it on sale. Three bars for nineteen cents."

The backchat relaxes them. Slightly.

They sit quietly, waiting to hear a hellacious racket. Oddly, they don't.

Harry briefs her on his save-the-world progress and seeing Peter Owen alive and well. He does not mention Maria Fernanda.

"Well, it sounds as if you started something with that slimy bookseller."

"I did my best to mess up his day. He got on the phone, but I didn't see Herr Wessel or the PVDE."

"Your English friend. What do you make of him?"

The Minox clinks against the gold ingot as Harry fishes it out of his pocket. "Peter's a player, but damned if I know why or how or what

115

or who. If he's missing his ingot of Nazi gold, he didn't complain. The Scotch either, which I thought he'd really miss."

It's cooling off and a breeze is coming in from the Rio Tejo. They look up at a sky sprinkled with stars.

Harry says, "I don't believe in God, you know. A good-guy God. He'd have to be a real crumb to invent Hitler."

"I know," she says. "I have my doubts too."

He points straight up and says, "That bright one there, it's either Venus or Mars."

She says, "If anybody believes in Martians, it's you."

"I do believe in Martians. Anybody who's ever been to an observatory has seen the canals. An astronomer named Percival Lowell discovered them around the turn of the century. His telescope wasn't strong enough to see the gondoliers, but they're there. You can count on it. They could have three heads, but they're on the job."

Dorothy's in no mood to debate him on the subject of space monsters. She'd be inviting Flash Gordon and Buck Rogers into the conversation, so she says nothing.

Harry puts an arm around her and says, "I'd offer you my jacket I don't have."

"My Sir Galahad," she says.

"I'm glad you dropped by."

She hesitates. "I told David I was exhausted and retiring early."

Harry's mind is on things other than spying, Peter, Martians, saving this planet, anything.

"Don't go away."

He returns to his building and is back in less than five minutes. "Nothing stirring, not even a Nazi."

"What did they do?"

"Also nothing, not even a cobweb was disturbed. Know what I think?"

"I've seldom known what you think."

"They were following you, not me."

"How?"

"They were probably following me, but lost me when I hopped a taxi from the Brasileira. Another team saw you leaving your hotel and got on your tail. This is Lisbon. Everybody's following everybody else. They didn't find you in my flat, and believed you'd slipped out a side door and are with me, which you are, though not out on the street, but here or we'd be in hot water."

"You didn't used to talk in circles like this, Harry. Not to this extent."

He takes her hand. "It's the only foreign language I'm fluent in."

"I've heard five or six tongues in this city, and we've just arrived."

"That's why I don't bother to learn foreign languages. It's too confusing. C'mon."

They reverse direction to his flat, Dorothy a little more comfortable on the ladder. Once inside, Harry props a chair against the door and says, "It's not safe for you to be outside again tonight."

"Am I a mind reader or did I know you were going to say that?"

Harry answers by digging through a tiny closet jammed to the gills with clothing he'd never wear and miscellaneous junk he'd forgotten his landlady hadn't bothered with. He hauls out a wind-up Victrola. He gives it a crank and puts on Duke Ellington.

"My dance floor is too small to jitterbug on. It'll have to be a slow number. May I have this dance?"

"There's not much room to dance to a slow one either."

"Fine by me."

They're barely into the second tune when she takes charge and pulls him onto the bed. Harry offers no resistance. Lust and adrenaline have made him dizzy.

"It's been a long time," he whispers.

"Too long."

His hand is under her dress, feeling the seam of her silk stocking, reaching for her garter.

"Let me help you," she says, turning her head.

Her cheek is on the pillow as she pulls her garter down.

She freezes, tenses.

"What am I smelling?"

"What are you smelling?"

"Perfume!"

Harry smells it too. Uh oh. Maria Fernanda's. He loves her perfume, but now the fragrance is *Eau de Oh Shit*.

He moves a hand inside Dorothy's panties, nuzzling her. "It's not perfume. It's the soap the laundry uses."

Dorothy jerks his hand out of her lingerie and sits up. "You liar."

"I swear —"

"I couldn't care less if you've slept with every tramp in Portugal, Horatio Alger, but you could have afforded me the common decency of changing your linen."

Before he can devise a lie or an excuse she hadn't heard before from him, or protest that her visit was a surprise, catching him when he was leaving for the laundry, Dorothy resets her unmentionables and turns on her side.

"Please get out of this bed and *good night*."

Harry finds a semi-clean pillowcase for her, an extra blanket for himself, and curls up on the rock-hard floor. He's getting mighty tired of the fetal position.

One woman plus one woman equals zero women: $W + W = 0$.

This is arithmetic he hadn't learned in *Dick and Jane*.

CHAPTER 15

In the morning, as if nothing had happened last night—which, as far as Harry is concerned, tragically nothing had—they eat a quiet breakfast at a small café at the base of Alfama, on a street parallel to the arch that leads into Praça do Comercio. They have eggs, toast and pastries and drink strong Brazilian coffee.

Harry had convinced Dorothy that the coast is clear, and even if it isn't, he does persuade her that Americans are not to be toyed with, not in public in broad daylight, surrounded by people. Nobody is that reckless and stupid, not even the PVDE.

Dorothy says, "We understood that all European capitals were short on all foodstuffs, but this bounty remains hard to believe, everything in Europe considered."

Harry says, "Lisbon and Stockholm are sitting pretty. There's a rumor that sugar is going to be rationed and butter runs short sometimes. But not cornflakes."

"Excuse me?"

"A guy I ran into a month or two ago has an expat buddy in Madrid. The buddy was homesick for cornflakes, so the guy scrounged five boxes here and sent them off. They cost three times the price at home at the A & P, but he was tickled pink."

"You could write a book," she tells him.

"Nobody would believe me. Are you going to eat that croissant?"

Dorothy had fluffed her hair, brushed her skirt with her hands and looks fresh as a daisy. Harry is disheveled and walks like a cripple, but had been smart enough not to complain or change clothes in front of her.

After the cornflakes story, there is a silence that Harry breaks with academically-tinged small talk. He lectures again about where they are, the Baixa, a perfect grid of streets that the Marquês de Pombal built after the 1755 earthquake.

Dorothy wants to tell him he's being repetitive, but prefers the sound of her own silence. Which doesn't last as she observes the parade of people coming and going, some looking at them.

"It's occurred to me that we're sitting here in front of God and everybody," she says. "Even though you imply the more the merrier, considering all the people who want a piece of your hide, is this wise? I feel like a sitting duck."

Harry flicks a dusting of powdered sugar from his crumpled shirt and says, "I think we're safe for three good reasons. Number one, trailing you is a higher priority than getting even with me. I'm a Judas goat."

"Aren't I?"

"Nope. Dorothy, your major-appliance selling brother is a secret agent and you're along as a science wizard."

Dorothy shakes her head unconvincingly.

"Okay. Back to my reasons. Number two, I may be worth more to them alive than dead."

"That's comforting. Why?"

"The mystery gold."

"Not politics in any way, shape or form?"

"Nope."

"The gold is in your pocket for the taking."

"Even if they have X-ray vision that detects gold, it's the beginning of the rainbow, not the end."

"I'm trying to make sense out of what you're saying, Harry."

"So am I."

"Are you going to lead them to that pot of gold?"

"Mox nix. I have to find it first. Number three. Look around us. As I've been trying to convince you, there are people here and at other close-by cafés. With so many witnesses, absolutely nothing's going to hap—"

He's interrupted by the screeching roar of a tan Buick that comes flying around the corner on two wheels, horn blaring, sending people scattering and diving for cover, tables tipping over, chinaware shattering. A gun barrel protrudes from a back window.

"Shit," Harry says as he lunges and throws himself on Dorothy, falling to the pavement atop her just as a bullet shatters his coffee cup.

"Harry—"

"You're all right."

"Let's get the hell out of here. We've worn out our welcome," he says, up on his knees as the Buick careens around the next corner and out of sight.

"Where? And don't say where the coast is clear."

"Elsewhere," he says, helping her to her feet.

Harry leads her past screaming employees and diners through the café, into the kitchen, smelling *sardinhas* and *bacalhau* (dried cod), the Portuguese national dishes. Out the back door, they enter a street as narrow as a sidewalk. They run up stairs and onto an even-narrower street that leads down a steep hill.

"The Casbah," Dorothy says.

"We sure could use Buck Rogers' invisibility ray."

"Harry, grow up."

"No time for that."

"Where are we going?"

"Home sweet home for you."

They go through a back door of another restaurant, into a janitor area and kitchen, ignoring Portuguese cursing, and onto a street that leads out to the Rossio.

Into the Hotel Metropole they hurry, Harry nearly plowing into and through the doorman as if he were a rival lineman.

"Heil Fucking Hitler," Harry tells him.

Whoever is pulling whom was unclear as they take the stairs two at a time.

David Booth swings open the door before Dorothy can touch it with her key.

Harry says, "Gee, sorry, Dad. I know I promised to have her home by ten. Had a flat tire on the jalopy."

"Get in here, you two!"

Dorothy obeys contritely.

Harry obeys, pretending to be contrite.

Holding a notepad, David has that clenched-chin, eyes-narrowed look to him that makes it difficult for Harry to resist telling him to shove his Phi Beta Kappa key so far up his ass that he can taste metal.

Dorothy says, "David, not fifteen minutes ago, Harry saved my life."

"Mine too," Harry says.

"Before you provide all the embellished details, Harry, do you recall an incident in Berlin on November 9, 1938?"

Harry touches his lips with a finger, reminding David that they have to go to the window and whisper, so they do.

"It's hard to forget for a history major such as myself. It was *Kristallnacht.*"

"I am not referring to a chapter in a textbook, Antonelli. Our Embassy has received an irate call from the Portuguese Foreign Ministry, their equivalent of the State Department, relaying an irate message from the German Embassy. It was indirect because we haven't been on speaking terms with Germany since they trampled Czechoslovakia."

"Yeah?"

"You've just been identified as a fugitive wanted for, and I quote, 'viciously, intentionally, and unlawfully attacking an innocent German citizen named Otto Krapphol.' Is that name familiar to you?"

"Nope. I'd remember a name like that."

"You've recently been identified."

Giving his wallet ID to Horst Wessel, goddamnit.

"It's a case of mistaken identity."

"I'm certain you will recall Herr Krapphol. He's the Nazi vandal you kicked in the groin during that melee you so often and colorfully describe."

"Him and seven others were all over me."

"How many?" Dorothy says.

"Otto Krapphol," David coaxes.

"I didn't catch his name. We don't exchange Christmas cards."

"He's the son of a high-ranking Party member and an elite contributor in the Lebensborn program. The father is an SS-Brigadeführer, the equivalent of a major general."

"They can stick their Lebensborn you know where."

"As loathsome as that regime and their policies are, we do have to get along with Prime Minister Salazar, who, in case you haven't noticed, is walking a neutrality tightrope. They further accuse you of being a fifth columnist in the employ of the British."

"Jeez, that fifth column thing again. Spain, now here. All I did was give three assholes swimming lessons. And if I'm in the employ of anybody, I haven't seen a paycheck lately, just a paltry handful of escudos."

"Have you blown all that money already?" Dorothy says.

David touches his lips, reminding Harry to stop yelling, and refers to his notes. "This is old news, but they also complain that you blew up a government staff car with a bomb."

"How many times do I have to tell you? I accidentally shot a hole in the gas tank. The sights were cockeyed on the Kraut's Luger."

Dorothy says, "Harry fired wildly at a tire, David. I'm fortunate he didn't hit me."

Harry nods vigorously.

David looks at his sister, then at Harry.

"I hate to lecture," Harry lectures, "You know what Lebensborn is all about, don't you, David? It's raising the Aryan birthrate by encouraging SS members to hatch babies with Aryan dames. What it means is they have free rein to fu... have intimate relations with and even rape plump, blue-eyed blondes, even if the poor gals have a headache at the time."

David Booth sighs. "Regardless, there's an open warrant on you by the PVDE. Portugal, I repeat, being neutral, is on a tenuous tightrope. They have to respond to the complaint."

"That pill at the waterfront you dunked," Dorothy says.

"I was a dodo to show him my ID without putting up a fuss. That's for sure."

"He had a gun on you," Dorothy says. "It was understandable."

David says, "Have I heard the whole story about this castration business?"

"Long story. Berlin was a hellhole," Harry says. "I was outnumbered ten to one and did what I had to do."

"Ten?" David says. "I thought it was seven."

Dorothy laughs. "Harry, you're a walking, talking, drinking, brawling international incident. You shouldn't be seen as well as not heard."

"Five to one. Seven. Ten. I had no time to count heads, only bust them. I put one out of commission by booting him in the nuts. Evidently our boy Otto. He was ready to brain me with a lead pipe."

"He's obviously the one," David says. "He required lifesaving surgery due to internal bleeding. Certain parts had to be amputated."

"He asked for it. I rest my case. I made life easier for Berlin blondes. If Otto showed up as a blind date, any dame who wasn't blind would—"

"Please be quiet and listen," Dorothy says.

"Next they'll be saying I tried to kill Hitler."

"Harry."

David says, "Did you?"

"Never had the opportunity. Now that you mention it, America has plenty of dough. Pay somebody to bump off Hitler," Harry says. "That'll end a whole bunch of problems."

"Thank you for your expert advice on foreign affairs," David says, "This is hush-hush, but as a side note there have been attempts on Adolf Hitler's life, a life that seems to be charmed. Our intelligence had revealed that German Army generals have conspired to launch a coup d'état."

"So why aren't we reading about that in the paper?"

"The old aristocratic generals despise this vulgar corporal who fought in the Great War, a homicidal maniac with bad table manners, but for various reasons it hasn't happened and at this point we doubt that it will."

"They've had certain parts amputated too, huh?"

Dorothy laughs.

Harry says, "I'm still not understanding the fuss. These birds are a dime a dozen."

"Need I repeat, your eunuch's father is a major general in the SS?"

Harry smiles and says, "In my opinion, every gelded Nazi is a plus."

"Agreed, but I'm only concerned in how this affects our mission and the political ramifications to it. The unwelcome attention."

"Yeah, your mission. Selling stoves and ice boxes. Right, Dave?"

"Please stay within the bounds of what we ask you to do, Harry," David says.

"Makes sense. As you intimated, more people in Lisbon are looking for me than not."

"You have an incredibly important mission, Antonelli. Can you please focus on that instead of participating in one hair-raiser after another?"

"If you can use some of your influence and get some of these people off my back, it sure would help me save the world."

"Once again, I'm not here officially," David says. "I have no official influence. I can do nothing but keep an eye on you and apparently I have failed."

"You've never failed at anything, Dave."

"Have you made headway at the Nazi bookstore?"

"Sure have."

"How?"

Harry tells him what he told Dorothy last night about the bookshop sissy and Peter Owen's reappearance. "Being shot at, isn't that headway too?"

David considers what he's been told. "If they wanted you dead now, I doubt if they would have missed."

"My thought too and I'm relieved," Harry says.

Dorothy says, "We were at point-blank range from that car."

Then again, Harry thinks. His coffee cup was one second from being at his lips.

"Other progress?"

Harry replies by rocking a hand. "Well, I gave the Nazi bookshop guy ants in his pants, which has to be connected with those birds ruining our breakfast, don't you think? They'll make another move."

"We have to be the impetus, not them."

Harry says, "I don't know. Impetus isn't necessarily the best approach if they have what they have and all we have is good intentions."

Dorothy says, "I have an idea."

David looks Harry up and down. "You can use a shower and a change while my sister and I talk."

CHAPTER 16

In the shower, Harry is hypnotized by the luxury, the shiny tile and chromium hardware, the finest soap, and hot water that runs forever. The last time he experienced such self-indulgence was in a bath with the Hungarian countess, him and her and bubbles overflowing the tub. If she was real or fake royalty, it didn't matter. That Magda was a few years his senior was an understatement. She was on the edge of middle age, a woman who'd been around, a dedicated teacher to Harry, who was eager to learn Magda's favorite subject.

Thinking of Magda and thinking that there's ample room in the shower for Dorothy to join him, Harry has a boner and a half.

It wilts at the sound of brother and sister arguing, exchanging louder yes's and no's, specifics wisely hushed. When they were kids, Harry remembers, Dorothy won the majority of their screamers, due mostly to perseverance.

When Harry comes out wrapped in a towel, Dorothy is in her room and David has clothes laid out on the Victorian torture sofa. The look on his face indicates that his sis came out on top again.

David says, "I thank my lucky stars I brought these articles along as a contingency. Disguising you crossed my mind, but I didn't think I'd be forced to do so this soon. Not that I approve. I don't want to know how she knew, but Dorothy remembered your sizes."

Harry leaves that one alone.

David turns his back as Harry obediently dresses in gray pinstripes, white shirt and tie.

David hands him a pair of flat-lens glasses, and two bottles.

"All this, standard issue for spies, huh?"

"Comb these solutions in. They'll darken your hair and give you gray highlights too. It'll mature you. Superficially."

Harry frowns. "I look like a Wall Street lawyer."

"Fantasize that you're a disbarred one under indictment, if that'll make you feel any better."

"Yeah, okay. I am a lot more comfortable now," he says in front of an ornate mirror.

Dorothy comes out of her room in a black skirt and white blouse that reveals nothing. Flat-lenses too. Harry stares at her, thinking: *You aren't just along for the ride. You're on Uncle Sam's payroll. No question.*

"You look like you escaped from a monastery," he tells her. "As a pair, we come off as missionaries. Who have sinned. And sinned and sinned."

Dorothy sticks out her tongue at him.

David looks at his sister. "Against my better judgment, you'll accompany him. The idea of your get-up is to make you appear harmless. Harry, for you that's a reach, but I must admit that as a pair you're quite bland."

"Bland is a new wrinkle for me," Harry says, adjusting his tie. "What's the plan?"

"You'll antagonize the bookstore Nazi and make him believe that a group of people is a threat, not just you. By yourself, Antonelli, you were unable to flush him out."

Harry looks at a mirror behind the tortuous sofa. "I don't know, Dave."

"If you show your face again soon, it'll have to be a new face and this is the best I can do. We need you out there. I'll conjure up a lie to the Embassy. Please get to work. Go into that bookshop. I'm at a loss for other ideas."

"And?" Harry says.

"Improvise."

"I wonder if they have autographed copies of *Mein Kampf* I can swoon over. It'll be a great test of our costumes," Dorothy says.

Not one to ever enthuse about David's schemes, he's all aboard on this one. But if all Secret Agent Dave has is Harry's improvisation, the world's in trouble.

"Dieter is fun and games. You'll love him, Dorothy. It'll be hate at first sight."

Dorothy says, "Let's light a bonfire under his oily backside and see where he runs."

"And please try to keep the authorities out of it," David says.

"A fool's errand," Harry thinks out loud. "Half-baked disguises and no firm plan."

The Booths look at him.

"What else do we have?" David says.

Harry opens the door for Dorothy and says, "I'll try not to take that personally, Dave."

CHAPTER 17

Dieter watches the couple closely as they enter and browse his bookshop. He cannot swear to it, but he thinks he saw them earlier at a corner café looking in his direction, and here they are less than a minute after his last customer departed. They strike him as missionaries, the strident sort that stand on sidewalk corners and push their cartoonish pamphlets on passersby. There is something familiar about the man too.

I am too good for this.

Dieter has been transferred here against his will from the Hamburg university where he taught rhetoric, ostensibly for his linguistic skills, his fluency in Portuguese and four other languages. Behind his back, they wanted him out for excessive self-aggrandizement and didacticism.

His letters demanding to be given an end date to this dismal assignment have gone unanswered. Dieter is realizing after the fact how unpopular he was at the university.

Whatever they have said about him, they will eat their words when he is recognized as the greatest German novelist in history! Kafka, Mann, Döblin, Roth—Jews, traitors, and in comparison to him, semiliterate dunces.

Götterdämmerung of Glory, when finished at long last, will outsell any tome but the divine *Mein Kampf*. It is to be a multigenerational tale of Germany's greatest rulers—Barbarossa, Bismarck, von Hindenburg and others—inserting the *Führer* in their places, hypothesizing what Adolf Hitler's leadership and wisdom would have meant for the Aryan people.

Dieter had been cautioned by faculty peers and present superiors that anything in the realm of propaganda must be approved, but he retorts, perhaps too snappishly to people too powerful, that his novel will be patriotic *literature*, thus immune from outside approval.

He trails discreetly as the suspicious couple goes to a corner niche he has reserved for Dr. Joseph Goebbels, photographs of him and his speeches bound in book form. In Dieter's view, Dr. Goebbels ranks among the greatest intellectuals throughout history. The only flaw in his thinking is that his book burnings excluded Western nursery rhymes and Mother Goose tales, each crammed with seditious allegories and rejection of authority.

Harry picks up a framed photo of the Nazi Minister of Propaganda.

Dorothy nudges him as he starts to speak and says to Dieter, "Do you have any autographed pictures of Mr. Herr Hitler or his wonderful book?"

"Oh, how I wish we did have signed copies," he rhapsodizes, soft, pudgy hands to his bony chest. "The *Führer* can do only so much."

Dorothy sighs theatrically. "Is Mister Hitler married? He is *so* adorable."

An American, Dieter wonders? A nation filled with uncivilized mixed breeds and assertive women who have forgotten their place.

"No he is not, *fräulein*. As the *Führer* explains so articulately, he cannot devote himself to a woman. He is married to Germany."

A heavier sigh. "That is womankind's loss."

"You are from where, if I may ask?"

"Canada. We're third-generation Germans."

"You do not have a German accent."

"We were assimilated. However, we're charter members of the German American Bund. We take a ferry across the lake from Toronto to Buffalo. The meetings are inspiring. We do great work at home spreading the word about the correct path Americans should follow, Roosevelt and his Communist lackeys be damned."

Dieter smiles at her. If he were capable of being sexually stimulated by a male or female, she could be the one.

Harry smiles at her, admiring her off-the-cuff bullshit.

Dorothy smiles back at him and winks, a signal that she has cut his leash.

Harry picks up a picture of Goebbels and says, "Hey, Frit-, uh, Dieter, do you have any circus pictures of him?"

"I beg your pardon?"

"Yeah. The deformed little lunatic in the big tent. Isn't he in scenes in that tent with the two-headed calf and the bearded lady?"

That voice, the deformed Semitic nose.

"You."

"In the flesh, Hans."

"Forgive him," Dorothy says, holding a *Mein Kampf,* which are stacked and shelved everywhere. "He knows not what he says."

The shopkeeper takes Dorothy's money, puts her purchase in a paper bag, and tells her, "Abandon him, *fräulein.* He is trouble."

He gives her change and the Nazi salute.

"*Heil Hitler!*"

"Oh goodness. You have perspiration marks under your armpits, Herr Dieter," Dorothy says. "Abandon that shirt to the garbage."

Harry gives him his middle-finger version and takes out the Minox.

"Smile," he says, clicking the shutter.

Outside, Dorothy says, "You were an unconvincing Canadian Nazi, Harry. You flopped at the end."

"I tried. My busted snout is like a set of fingerprints."

"What are we going to do with this horrid book? My hands feel dirty touching it."

"Emergency toilet paper."

They loiter at the next corner long enough to see the bookstore Nazi stroking his nose while on the phone.

Dorothy raises to her tiptoes and kisses Harry's damaged schnoz. "I should have known—that was the Achilles' heel of your getup."

The bar behind them is opening its doors.

Harry says, "It's not too early for a pick-me-up."

"Not the sort you have in mind, mister, but you can buy me an early lunch."

Her coffee and his whiskey are on their table when a tan Buick pulls up to the bookstore.

"Oh no, the same car?"

Harry says, "There's a Buick dealership in town, so maybe, maybe not. I didn't have time to get the license number of our last one."

Out of the left rear seat strides Horst Wessel.

"Crazy Horst doesn't mind who sees him, does he?" Harry says.

"Especially us," Dorothy says.

Wessel pauses to sneeze and goes inside.

"Oh dear, Harry. You may have given him pneumonia."

"You should never go in the water with your clothes on. I learned that in YMCA swim class."

They watch Wessel listening to the frenzied, gesticulating shopkeeper, who frequently touches his nose and makes eyeglasses with his fingers.

"That seals the deal," Harry says. "Your brother would never make a living in Hollywood, making up the actors."

"We should've done you as a hunchback of Notre dame, Harry."

The pair rush out to a car door immediately opened by the Buick's driver. Dieter first locks up his store, then gets in with Wessel, and off they go. Slowly.

"How come they're not in an all-fired hurry?" Harry says.

Dorothy says, "Finish your drink. On second thought, don't."

"Dick Tracy and Tess Trueheart, that's us."

"Will you stop that, Harry? I mean it."

Harry tosses the *Mein Kampf* in the nearest garbage receptacle and hails a taxi.

CHAPTER 18

Once upon a time, in the German city of Halle, near Leipzig, Reinhard Tristan Eugen Heydrich was born on March 7, 1904. He was raised in a cultured, musical environment. His father founded the Halle Conservatory of Music and was a Wagnerian opera singer, while his mother was an accomplished pianist. Young Reinhard trained seriously as a violinist, developing good skills, and a lifelong passion for the violin.

At home Heydrich's mother believed in the value of harsh discipline and frequent lashings. As a result, Heydrich was a withdrawn, sullen boy, unhappy, but also intensely driven to excel. As he grew he excelled at academics and also displayed natural athletic talent, later becoming an award-winning fencer.

Too young to serve in World War One, after the war at age sixteen, Heydrich teamed up with a local right-wing, anti-Semitic organization of ex-soldiers involved in violent street fighting against Communists. Heydrich was also influenced by the racial fanaticism of the German *Völk* movement and its belief in the supremacy of the blond-haired, blue-eyed Germanic people which he resembled. He took delight in associating with these groups to disprove the persistent, but false rumors regarding his possible Jewish ancestry, presumably brought about by his prominent proboscis.

In March of 1922, at age eighteen, Heydrich sought the free education, adventure and prestige of a Naval career and became a cadet. Heydrich was by now over six feet tall, a gangly, awkward young man who had a high, almost falsetto voice. Fellow cadets took delight in calling him "Billy Goat" because of his bleating laugh and taunted with "Moses Handel" because of rumored Jewish ancestry and his unusual passion for classical music.

A seething, embittered Heydrich persevered and rose by 1926 to the rank of second lieutenant, serving as a signal officer attached to Intelligence. The teasing and taunting soon gave way to resentment over the extraordinary arrogance of this young man who was already dreaming of becoming an admiral.

Heydrich also developed an interest in women and pursued sex with the same driven desire for achievement he applied to everything else. He had many sexual relationships and in 1930 was accused of hiding the bratwurst with an unmarried daughter of a shipyard director. According to popular Nazi legend, in 1931, as a result of his refusal to marry her, Heydrich was forced to resign his commission for "conduct unbecoming to an officer and a gentleman."

With his Naval career shattered, his fiancée, an enthusiastic Nazi Party member, suggested he join the Party and look into the SS organization which, at that time, served mainly as Hitler's personal bodyguard and had about 10,000 members. In 1931, at age 27, Heydrich joined up and did become accepted in the SS, the elite organization of black-shirted young men chosen on the basis of their racial characteristics and psychotic personalities.

An interview was set up with the new SS *Reichsführer*, Heinrich Himmler, who was seeking someone to build an SS intelligence service. Himmler was impressed by Heydrich's Aryan looks, self-confidence, and unruffled justification of evil, and gave him the job. Heydrich proceeded to create the intelligence gathering organization known as the SD or SS Security Service.

Heydrich quickly grew the organization into a vast network of informers that developed dossiers on anyone who might oppose Hitler and conducted internal espionage and investigations to gather information down to the smallest details on Nazi Party members and storm trooper (SA) leaders.

Heydrich also had a taste for gossip and maintained folders full of rumors and details of the private lives and sexual activities of top Nazis, later resorting to planting hidden microphones and cameras. This recipe of ambition and ruthlessness soon moved him to the top ranks of the Nazi party.

*****

Reinhard Heydrich's pleasant sojourn to Lisbon is not entirely business. He has enjoyed an entertaining day and has accomplished much for the Reich. With details attended to, he is relaxing, basking in his own glory.

This radioactivity project, *his* project, when it succeeds, will win the *Führer's* heart. He may even leapfrog Himmler to Number Two. Himmler who kills by mere hundreds and thousands. A handful, in Heydrich's opinion.

A million *Engländers* in one blow dying in anguish. Two million. Three million. Eight million! And if something befalls the *Führer*, who better to replace Him? Reinhard Heydrich, architect of the Final Solution, the man a colleague had said for whom truth and goodness has no intrinsic meaning.

SS *Obergrupperführer* Reinhard Heydrich—the Hangman, the Butcher of Prague, the Blond Beast—is thinking this as he often does. He had flown to Lisbon in the predawn in the *Führer's* own airplane and visited the secret laboratory. The Jew scientist developing the radioactive compound had pissed himself at the sight of Heydrich and nearly fainted when asked if the powder could be made "Jew-specific," a delightful reaction.

Who says I lack a light, comical side?

The scientist did convince Heydrich and his entourage that acceptable progress is being made on the secret weapon. If desired, an airplane fitted with extra fuel tanks could conceivably be flown

136

one-way on a suicide mission to New York City or Washington, DC. After the devastation of London, America is an intriguing target to consider. If millions of New Yorkers and Washingtonians are eliminated, they will be made aware of the futility of resistance and sue for peace even before declaring war. *Lebensraum*, or living space, is constantly on the *Führer's* mind. Where better than vast America? Their limitless supply of natural and industrial resources. Of well-educated slave labor and Aryan women too.

Heydrich is satisfied and will continue to fund the project. If gold is required beyond banknotes, the responsibility is his, Hitler has informed him. The Reich requires gold for expenses to maintain soldiers on the ground, airmen and submariners. While the experimental radiation poison is appealing, it is experimental and unproven, the *Führer* cautions repeatedly. He demands results and He demands them soon.

Heydrich understands and accepts the *Führer's* wisdom. With Portuguese tungsten laundered into gold via the Swiss money whores, funding should be adequate. After the mission is accomplished, the laboratory will be razed and all personnel liquidated, so what concern is finance to them?

The *Führer* will be mightily pleased, as will Himmler.

Reinhard Heydrich is shaped like an elongated pear, with a bullet head and a suspiciously Hebrew-esque honker. His disguise of double-breasted suit, dark glasses and fedora is essential, but overheating him.

This local drinking parlor, Café do Canção, is insufficiently cooled by ceiling fans. Horst Wessel, the obsequious SS agent at his side apologizes for this as he apologizes for any inconvenience, as if guarding against a swat.

Dieter Somebody, the mousy little bookstore man who resembles Himmler, had alerted Wessel regarding a meddlesome American, the prime suspect in unlawfully castrating the son of a high-ranking Party member and elite contributor in the *Lebensborn* program.

If he and the American cross paths, fine.

Of greater priority is locals who harbor Jews. This is an outrage. Wherever he or she is, Reinhard Heydrich's eyes and ears are open. In this bar, they are wide open.

A report through intelligence channels that the Americans are developing a light ray of some nature that will render its soldiers invisible? Since the uranium facility is the matter of focus, Heydrich is not going out of his way to search for answers to this pie-in-the-sky rumor.

Annoyingly, Horst Wessel is sticking to him like wallpaper paste. Local secret police are at nearby tables. Wessel is a faithful puppy, but this slavishness will not increase his lifespan. So privy to the project, he will have to go too, regardless of his devotion to the New Order.

This bookseller also, who speaks insanely of an idiotic novel he is writing until a withering stare from Heydrich puts an end to it. Inserting Adolf Hitler into historical events is presumptuous and reckless. Any fact and fancy regarding the *Führer* is in the purview of Dr. Goebbels and nobody else. Bookshop clerks are easy to replace. Dieter Somebody knows this, taking the hint, and taking his leave from the Canção before he further offends.

Heydrich is sick of Wessel's sneezing and sniffling too, his complaining of a chill and a head cold, and simultaneously congratulating himself for hanging a poster of the *Führer* on the wall beside Salazar's in this tawdry bar. It is one of Heydrich's favorites, however, of him at Nuremberg. God-like. There is no other way to characterize His greatness.

Heydrich drinks from a mug of good German beer, sips his jigger of whiskey, and looks around. These Portuguese, they are an olive-skinned Mediterranean race with an African negroid derivation dating to the Moorish times in the Iberian Peninsula. He does not like being in their company.

After Germany annexes Spain and Portugal, he will eugenically evaluate them with Himmler. There is no room in the Third Reich for inferior races of any breed. Franco and Salazar are rulers friendly to Germany, but feel free to speak their minds. Annexation can and will change that. They will unequivocally comply with the Third Reich or else.

A devoted husband with four children, among his more human qualities, Reinhard Heydrich is a womanizing sexual psychopath and a mean drunk. He is feeling his liquor and liking what he sees on stage, the sultry woman singing the local simpering songs at this depressing hole in the wall. They could use accordions and an oompah sound to liven up this pitiful excuse for a beer hall.

The woman singer has been mentioned by Berlin. There are strong albeit unsubstantiated suspicions about her, that there is more to her than meets the eye, a possible Jewish connection at an unknown level. Heydrich has decided to make time to personally investigate her. He imagines what is inside her silken clothing.

"The American is here, *Obergruppenführer.*"

Heydrich says to Wessel, "The male American in question?"

A man like this with such a high, nasal voice, it is such a dichotomy, Wessel thinks. A man for the ages who, when excited, is an opera soprano.

"He just came in with the American woman who he was with when he defiled the German bookshop."

"I see him. This endless driving of yours was an excellent trap. As is your proposal that I have the opportunity to make his acquaintance here."

Horst Wessel glows, relieved, unable to speak. Reinhard Heydrich is demanding and unforgiving. He knows that if he fails this assignment, he can expect reassignment to Poland. Or worse.

"The American is cunning, sir. And foolhardy."

Heydrich waves a hand. "Business can wait. The girl on the stage. She comes first. Move the car somewhere inconspicuous, clear off the back seat, and have the police bring her to it."

139

"Shall they stand by, sir?"

"I have no need for security. The singer will learn to keep out of affairs that do not concern her and to know what a real man is like. If your American nemesis attempts to meddle, detain him. I shall arrange for his comeuppance later."

HISTORICAL NOTE: This conceit will cost Heydrich his life in a Prague hospital on June 4, 1942. On May 27, during his daily commute from home to office with light security, he is attacked by partisans.

The long-overdue final solution of Reinhard Heydrich will come 4½ months after Heydrich and others met to devise the Final Solution, the most barbarous powwow in history.

Heydrich smiles and actually enjoys the woman's music.

*****

Sitting at a Canção table, drinking Super Bock out of bottles, Dorothy and Harry are steamed.

They know they've been hoodwinked by the Nazis. Spending a small fortune on cab fare, they had trailed the Buick to a pastry café where the bookshop Nazi had killed time with Wessel, whereupon another Buick picked them up. On and on, from café to café until ten minutes ago.

"They baited the hook and we bit," Dorothy says. "Why here, I wonder? Is this a random choice of a stopping point?"

"They did and we did. Randomly. At this random stopping point," Harry says, alarm bells clanging inside his skull.

"What do we do?"

"Like we're doing, having a cold drink," Harry says. "I'm parched."

Dorothy asks Harry, "Who's Mata Hari up there singing that sad song?"

Harry shrugs. "Oh, her? Who knows? She's singing *fado,* the

Portuguese folk music. *Lisboa a Noite*, I think. It's a big hit, as big as Big Band tunes back home, like *Deep Purple* and *In the Mood*."

"Oh my God, are you crying?"

"It's the smoke."

She laughs. "Cigarette smoke bothers you? Since when?"

"Okay, something's caught in my eyes."

"Eyes? Oh, really? She's making goo-goo eyes at you, Antonelli."

"You're imagining things, Dorothy."

"Use your eyes."

"If she is, I hadn't noticed."

"Out with it. How well do you know her?"

Harry shrugs again, even less convincingly. "She is kind of familiar. I may have seen her sing here. They have a number of vocalists."

"You are familiar with this place. You're a regular, are you?"

"Not exactly."

"A little birdie tells me what her perfume choice is."

An astonished Harry looks at her. "Where the hell are you going with this? I'm not understanding."

Dorothy looks at Maria Fernanda and says, "I'll have to ask her where she buys the fragrance. If she does buy it or it's a gift from one of her lovers."

Harry ignores the badgering. If he's going to fight, it won't be with Dorothy. Not now, not in this room with these birds they've been trailing.

He says, "Okay, if you're gonna invent a connection between her perfume and me, I can't do anything about it. Haven't you heard that old saying, how it's better to forgive and forget?"

"I have to forget before I can forgive, Harry. And for the tenth time, that bookstore Nazi ran us all over town ending up here to draw us into a trap. He did his job and he's gone. Why?"

"Good question. Hey, that poster on the wall of Hitler, that's new."

"You've very observant. So you admit you are a regular."

"It's a small town. I may have been here three or four times. I don't remember. Hitler posters I remember."

Dorothy says, "I recommend we sit calmly and drink our beer, then report back to David."

"I can't go ahead with the mission unless I stick my neck out," he says.

"And have it chopped off. Half the audience is PVDE agents. You said so. I hear a sneeze."

"Horst Wessel in the horst flesh. He should do something about that cold. Who's the guy with him disguised as a guy in disguise?" Harry says, thinking that the town is one big Halloween party. "He looks kind of familiar."

"He does."

Lisboa a Noite ends to applause, Harry subduing his, grazing his eyes with his fingers, wiping a stray tear.

What the fucking hell. As Maria Fernanda leaves the stage, two PVDE types roughly escort her out the back door as she kicks at them and screams. Everybody ignores them.

The disguised guy in disguise follows.

The PVDE goons come back in.

Harry looks at Dorothy.

"Harry, don't."

Harry stands and says, "Who else will?"

He takes her non-reply as a green light. Walking fast but not too fast, he pauses at the Hitler poster. The goddamn thing offends the hell out of Harry. Like a turd in a punch bowl. Adolf's bug eyes don't follow him like Salazar's do; he's looking off into the distance, maybe to the Planet Mongo, which he may also have plans for after he conquers Earth.

Regardless, it doesn't belong here or anywhere else in neutral Lisbon. Harry tears it from the wall and carries it out the front door, wadding it as he races around the block.

The guy in disguise who looks like a guy in disguise is on the back seat of the Buick, on top of Maria Fernanda forcing his bulk between her legs.

"*Não, não, não!*"

One of Heydrich's hands is under her dress, tearing at her panties, the other on her throat. "Be quiet and enjoy me. All you whores like it."

She spits in his face. "I am no whore, you German pig."

He grinds against her. "You are a slut and you do other despicable things, you and your Jews. Tell me or you will not leave this car alive after we have had our fun."

Reinhard Heydrich releases her throat, so he can unbuckle his belt.

Harry sprints to the car faster than Jesse Owens (he thinks) and takes the guy by the ankles, but Portuguese agents and Wessel have been on alert. They rush there and peel Harry's hands loose, dragging him off by his heels.

"Do not take him far away," Heydrich orders them. "He is to be my audience. He can learn how a man treats a woman."

"Fuck you," Harry says, struggling as the agents jerk him closer to the car. "What's with your voice? You sound like a girl who got her tit caught in a wringer."

"Enjoy my fun, see how a real man does a whore," Heydrich says. "Then you will go for a ride. Your rude remark guarantees your death sentence."

"Says you," Harry says.

He yanks a hand free, grips the wadded poster with his teeth, and sets it on fire with his cigarette lighter.

"Put it out!" Wessel yells, watching and coughing.

Harry flings the burning poster at him and roundhouses a PVDE agent, dropping him. Wessel throws an arm around Harry's neck, choking him.

Harry is struck on the cheek by glass shards. Wessel howls and loosens his grip. Dorothy is in the corner of his eye, then not.

Harry spins and drives a fist into Wessel's gut.

Another PVDE type appears, delivering punches that clobber nothing but air.

Harry has become a dervish, Dick Tracy and the Phantom and Batman in one. With an uppercut, Harry drops the agent to a knee. Not one to kick somebody who's down, Harry makes an exception and kicks him twice.

Maria Fernanda Ramos is screaming and Reinhard Heydrich is breathing heavily. The *SS-Obergrupperführer* is so aroused that he doesn't hear the outside activity. He finishes releasing his belt buckle and grabs for the seat as he is being yanked out of the car, landing knees-first on the pavement.

Holding his trousers, Heydrich quickly gains his feet.

"American, who are you?"

"An American scientist who invented an invisibility ray."

"A stupid lie, American."

"Okay, I'm a guy who's gonna teach you some manners, Herr Fuckhead."

Heydrich says, "Wait for me to fasten my trousers so we can fight like gentlemen."

Ready for anything, Harry bows and says, "That is an honorable and reasonable request, sir. I will."

As Heydrich looks down to fasten his belt, before unchivalrous Harry can kick him in the teeth, Heydrich removes a dagger from his pocket and slashes wildly.

Harry jumps backward. The tip of the blade slices his shirt.

"So chivalry is dead, huh?" Harry says, sidestepping and driving a fist into Heydrich's ribs, knocking him into a car door.

Gasping, Heydrich swings the dagger horizontally, but Harry takes him by the wrist and twists it until Heydrich releases the dagger, then kicks the German in the back of his knees.

Maria Fernanda climbs out of the car, pulls up her panties, and runs off.

Bent over and holding his ribs. Heydrich looks at Harry. "You will pay for this."

"Fuck you, Hans. That's no way to treat a lady or a gentleman."

A skilled fighter, Heydrich recovers quickly and steps forward, fists balled. "You will beg me to stop and then you will tell everything."

Harry fakes a left jab. Heydrich cocks his head and whiffs with a right uppercut. Harry has the Minox out of his pocket and is squeezing it in his right hand, his impromptu brass knuckles.

He sidesteps and breaks the German's impressive nose with a right cross, sending his fedora and glasses flying. He drives a left into his gut and then a right, and smashes his left cheek with the hardest right he can muster.

The Blond Beast falls to his knees, nose bleeding profusely, retching and simultaneously soiling his pants.

A tan Buick bounds into the narrow street and men pile out, running to assist the fallen German.

"I can take a hint," Harry says, scramming.

In the darkness, Harry sees arms outstretched in his direction. If they aren't pointing guns at him, he's the Queen of Sheba.

"Good riddance to bad rubbish," Harry yells to no one, anyone and everyone as he turns the opposite corner, knees high, legs pumping.

He hears gunfire. A bullet whistles by his head.

"Harry!"

Holding a broken beer bottle, Dorothy is yelling and waving beside a car, rear door open. He hops into the back of a 1938 Ford sedan with her. David's in the front, behind the wheel. They squeal away from the curb as a PVDE bullet punctures a fender.

"My wondrous Wonder Woman."

"Use better sense, Antonelli," she says, tossing the beer bottle stem out her window. "I'm not going to make a habit of rescuing you from yourself."

"Okay, you talked me into it. The guy's not supposed to be the damsel in distress."

145

"Did you manage to snap a photo of anyone?" David says.

"I used the camera, but didn't get a snapshot."

"I don't understand."

"Long story,"

"We sure could use a picture as evidence."

Harry blows on his stinging knuckles. "Evidence of what?"

"Do you know who that is?" David says.

"He's familiar, maybe from pin-ups plastered all over Berlin, but we didn't have time for formal introductions."

David tells him, adding, "Even for a high-ranking Nazi, Reinhard Heydrich is a bad actor."

"He's probably not in Lisbon for the climate and the sardines," Harry says.

"Indeed not."

"Does that mean we're making progress or have another international incident on our hands?"

This is the first time Harry has heard David laugh out loud since they were kids, prior to his third-grade gold stars.

CHAPTER 19

Horatio Alger (Harry) Antonelli, skinned and bruised, recalcitrant man-child and general troublemaker, is stashed in the Booths' suite by orders of David, who has apologized himself hoarse on the telephone to various grandees, plenipotentiaries and wallahs, lying out of both sides of his mouth, citing mistaken identity when he thinks he can get away with it. When he can't, he argues that the skirmish was instigated by others who had provocatively displayed a large photograph of Adolf Hitler in a private establishment, in this, the city of Lisbon, *nouveau* City of Light, capital of neutral Portugal. Furthermore, lighting fire to the poster unreasonably stretches the definition of arson as it occurred under duress and out-of-doors.

Yes, he has conceded to embassies and consulates, it is not right and proper for a fugitive American to savagely beat a German tourist in Lisbon on holiday, nor his friends, nor government police officials. Although as a major appliance sales manager without portfolio, as a friend of Portugal and a supporter of Prime Minister Antonio Salazar's policies, David Booth will leave no stone unturned in his search for this individual, a demonstration of the best intentions.

The savagely-beaten German tourist is unnamed and unavailable. There has been no mention of Reinhard Heydrich by any party.

Harry has never been so proud of David Booth. He's showing a slippery, conniving, lying, devious side Harry has never before seen. He wisely keeps the kudos to himself.

Before the Booth siblings retire, they warn Harry to stay put.

"I talked myself hoarse, Antonelli," David says. "Entirely on your behalf. Do not go near that door."

Like confining a misbehaving child to his room.

"But it wasn't my fault," is Harry's rejoinder, as it was in childhood from the time he was old enough to speak.

David's cold rebuttal is silence and a bedroom-door slam behind him.

Harry does try to be good, but curled up on the Victorian sofa, Harry is unable to sleep. This Judas goat business is a mess and they're no closer to the deadly uranium. If there is any of the stuff.

Lisbon's population is approximately 750,000 plus tens of thousands of refugees. If any one of them know of a secret weapon, they ain't making a peep to anybody in any language. If Harry's gonna save the world, he can't find a haystack needle while on restriction.

He's thirsty, but the ice box contains only soda pop and a pitcher of water, not the thirst-quenchers he has in mind. Dying for a cigarette too, he gets off the torture device and stretches. The door locks by itself when one leaves the suite. He doesn't have a key and is smart enough not to ask for one.

Harry hears a scratching at the door, as if somebody's puppy has gotten loose. He opens it a couple of inches, to a whiff of halitosis and stale alcohol, and a hand with a lock pick in it.

"Harry, blimey, you are the dickens to find," Peter Owen says. "I was going to surprise you."

Fingertip to lips, Harry lets him in.

"People are sleeping," he whispers.

"Indeed. Most everybody but us are at this late hour."

"How the hell did you find me?"

"Not easily, I assure you. Ever since you ran out on me at the rear door of the pub and the fascists ripped apart me flat, I've been concentrating in making meself hard to find also, moving about like a bloody gypsy."

Harry points to an armchair. "Have a seat and keep your voice down. The room has a hidden microphone and my hosts are grouchy. And answer my question."

"Very well. I have nothing to conceal. I stopped at the Canção for a libation and witnessed the aftermath of a mad scene. I swear, every PVDE roughneck in Lisbon was in and about, spiriting a mugging victim off in the direction of the new airport they're building. An extremely important foreigner, I gather. I made inquiries of bystanders and fabricated a picture. Bystanders who were adequately calm to speak, that is. There was gunfire. A man fitting your description was taken away in a car to this general area. It wasn't difficult to narrow it down to you, Harry."

"Where's Maria Fernanda? How is she?"

"I didn't see her. Bystanders told of a woman being accosted, who was fortunate enough to escape a rapist's clutches. Her?"

Harry changes the subject. "The corks? A dead issue? I know the answer, but I have to ask. The dough would come in handy."

"Not a dead issue to the authorities who seized them. We can be sure of that. An income supplement, the items are, Harry."

Harry says nothing, thinking of the small fortune in his pocket. Even if he knew where to peddle it, he knows that he'll be in even hotter water if he tries.

Peter says, "I brought a treat, a peace offering if you remain in a snit and it sounds as if you are, believing incorrectly as you do that the songstress and I are a romantic duo. I swear, that bird and I are platonic friends."

Peter brings from behind his back a bottle of port.

"Nary an instant younger than twenty years, from Porto's finest winery. The grandest there is."

A mollified Harry finds two glasses and a corkscrew.

"A toast," Peter says after Harry fills their glasses.

Harry clinks Peter's and drinks, afraid to ask what they're toasting.

"Harry, what are you doing here with those people?"

"What people?"

"The bird and chap who have been seen around this hotel. They bear a family resemblance to each other," he says, pointing at the bedroom doors. "Are we hushing ourselves on their account?"

"Oh, them. They're old friends from my hometown who're touring parts of Europe Hitler hasn't gobbled up yet. They relieve my homesickness. By doing so, they're helping me to stay out of jail and out of the morgue. He's a major appliance sales director too, you know, trying to gain a foothold in Lisbon. He represents all the major brands. Westinghouse and GE and others."

Peter nods. "Highly laudable goals. Your General Electric and Frigidaire machines are respected worldwide."

"They're selling like hotcakes too," Harry says. "He can't get them shipped here fast enough."

"I recollect your mention of a German questioning you on the subject of gold. What became of that situation?"

How does Peter know? Did Harry let it slip? He's taken so many poundings lately that he mistrusts his memory.

"I wasn't lying when I said I didn't know about gold and it was a bulletin that he knew about you."

"If you have power, Lisbon is a small town, Harry." He reaches into a pocket. "This is the ultimate power."

Peter gives Harry a gold ingot the dimensions of a playing card, though thicker. Stamped on it: the German eagle, DEUTSCHE REICHSBANK, and a serial number. It's a double of the ingot in his pocket.

"Pure gold, Harry. Pure as the driven snow. Don't be put off by the swastika. It can be melted down. Gold is gold. In wartime, gold is a delectable concoction of guns *and* butter."

Harry hefts it. The ingot is properly heavy.

Playing innocent, he says, "Peter, where the hell did you find this?"

Fingertip to lips, Peter Owen says, "Quiet. Your people are sleeping."

"Peter. Where. The. Hell. Did. You. Get. This?"

"Ever hear the fable of Pandora's box?"

"Sure. I busted it open long ago."

Peter gets up. "Available for a little trip?"

"Where?"

Peter says, "To where this lovely metal is stacked to the ceiling."

Save the world or make some money?

Two dead birds, one stone?

When they leave, Harry is careful to shut the door quietly.

Outside the hotel, Harry turns to ask Peter where this cornucopia is.

Peter isn't there, but a tan Buick is, racing toward him.

That's when the lights go out.

CHAPTER 20

Harry Antonelli awakens, flat on his back, on the bench. The sky's overcast and snowflakes are falling on his face. The trainer is giving him smelling salts. It's late in the game in Pullman, Washington against Washington State College, their hated cross-state rival.

"What's the score?" Harry asks.

The trainer says, "It's seven to seven. They scored on us while you were out, sleeping beauty. Your man caught a nineteen-yard pass to tie the game."

HISTORICAL NOTE: On October 9,1937, too early for a single snowflake, Washington and Washington State did play to a 7-7 tie, despite the UW dominating in yards gained, 295 to 154. Harry Antonelli had no impact on the result. Pullman, The population of Pullman Washington, was an estimated 4,000: 14,581 attended the football game.

But Harry Antonelli is not in 1937 Pullman, he's in 1940 Lisbon. He's not on his back either. He's awakening flat on his stomach in the back seat of the Buick, hands bound tightly with cord, and a PVDE heavyweight sitting on his legs.

"Sorry, mate," Peter says, in front as the driver grinds through the gears. "It's either you or me. Those were the choices presented to me, who, like yourself, as we have oft said, is a charter member of the Me, Myself and I Party."

"You and your phony non-accent. I knew a guy from Deadwood, South Dakota, whose voice is a dead ringer for yours."

"Only one time zone apart, mate. Keokuk, Iowa."

"Corn as high as an elephant's eye. Sunday band concerts."

"I don't miss it for an instant, laddie."

"I'm sure you don't, wherever you're really from. Who the fuck are you, Peter?"

"I'm nobody, Harry, and everybody. I'm a chippy who drops his knickers and spreads his legs for the promise of a dollar, an escudo, a peseta, a pound, a mark, a franc or a lira. Or a train ticket out of town if circumstances dictate."

"You and Maria Fernanda?"

"Too complicated to answer in the limited amount of time we have."

"The demolition of your flat was staged, wasn't it? Otherwise, I'd never've found the ingot."

"Alas, my whiskey too. A sacrificial offering to you, my dearest friend."

"You – !"

"I am all those things and less, chum."

The Buick slams to an abrupt halt. Harry's torso twists, but his legs don't. It does nothing for his headache.

Peter gets out. Someone else gets in and sneezes.

The door had been held open for the new passenger by bookshop Dieter who yells a shrill curse in German in Harry's ear.

The car door slams and off they go.

"I do not swim today," says a familiar voice in front of him. "You may later, however, in your clothes and with restraints, like Harry Houdini."

For lack of a witty response, Harry says, "Fuck you, Herr Wessel."

Wessel sniffles and laughs.

"You really oughta take care of that cold, Wessel. I recommend chicken soup with strychnine."

"Allow me to sing you a lullaby. You can rest as we drive. It may make your fate easier to endure."

"Save your voice."

In a scratchy tenor, Horst Wessel sings the Nazi anthem, *The Horst Wessel Song*:

> *The flag on high! The ranks tightly closed!*
> *The SA marches with quiet, steady step.*
> *Comrades shot by the Red Front and reactionaries*
> *March in spirit within our ranks.*
> *Clear the streets for the brown battalions,*
> *Clear the streets for the storm division!*
> *Millions are looking upon the swastika full of hope,*
> *The day of freedom and of bread dawns!*
> *For the last time, the call to arms is sounded!*
> *For the fight, we all stand prepared!*
> *Already Hitler's banners fly over all streets.*
> *The time of bondage will last but a little while now!*
> *The SA march with quiet, steady step.*
> *Comrades shot by the Red Front and reactionaries,*
> *March in spirit within our ranks.*

Harry says, "A catchy number. I can see Hitler dancing to it in a pink tutu."

"You may not be around to see the *Führer* after he has conquered Europe. You may not think that is so funny. If you are lucky enough to survive the night, rather than a moonlight swim, you may be sent to a camp to be with all your Jew friends."

Harry says, "Hitler was gassed in the Great War. Too bad we didn't finish the job on the maniac. A pest exterminator with rat poison is just the ticket."

"Silence!"

"Have you made an appointment with Doctor Freud yet, Wessel?

You're nuttier than ever."

"After the evening is through, you will be begging us to throw you into the Rio Tejo like you did me."

"Don't count your chickens yet, Wessel," Harry threatens without conviction.

Harry feels a *thump thump thump* of a wooden pier underneath as he listens to Horst Wessel's laughter.

CHAPTER 21

The car stops with a painful jolt and Harry hears a sliding door roll up. He is yanked out onto his feet and roughly ushered into a long, narrow building. His head is lolling, and he has to be half-carried, half-dragged. The car drives off and the door rolls shut. The smell is no-smell and there are no outside sounds, not even a ship's whistle, odd for this close to the Rio Tejo, Harry thinks. The place has to be jam-packed with asbestos insulation.

Harry can blurrily distinguish numerous partitions. Lighting is steady and low intensity. A humming sound seems to come from the rear.

Another chapter in a weird day, Harry thinks. Hopefully not his last.

A small man in a white lab coat accompanied by men in business suits are out front, waiting. The suited individuals hold Lugers at their sides, not a welcome sight to a man terrified by guns. They look angry and eager to do mayhem. The guy in the lab coat is wiry, gaunt. He has curly hair and thick glasses. He is not holding a Luger and he appears to be scared to death of guns and most else.

"Where the hell are we?" Harry mumbles, trying his best to recover his equilibrium.

He's slapped on the back of the head, a clue that they don't want him to speak unless spoken to. Him the guest of honor it seems.

Harry is coming out of his torpor, faking wooziness, his head continuing to droop as he steadily digs his fingernails in and loosens the cord binding his wrists.

Horst Wessel had entered first and is standing behind the small man. He too is holding a Luger, a replacement for the one with the faulty sights that had caused the car fire and explosion. Harry cannot bear to focus on it.

The goon who had been sitting on Harry's legs in the car shoves him forward. Harry stumbles and pretends to nearly lose his balance.

Horst Wessel says, "You are at the dawn of a new civilization, Antonelli. You and the esteemed Jew scientist are going to launch a new era for the Fatherland."

This has to be where they're brewing the poison uranium, the mad scientist and all his pals, David's target. Too bad Dave can't be here. Along with an armored division.

His wits and balance fully restored, Harry begins to fall, to gauge the reaction speed of his captors, but is assisted by a goon with a grunt and a jerk. "Always glad to be helpful, Hans. How am I gonna launch your fucked-up Fatherland?"

"First, you will tell us where the gold is."

"What gold?"

"Gold that is required to continue our sacred mission."

"What gold that is required to continue what sacred fucking mission, Fritz?"

"As much as we would love to enjoy your horror, we have no time to explain and to encourage your cooperation. The fruit of our labor is ready for transport. There is risk in doing so, risk that you will undertake for us. Tell us where the gold is and you may be allowed to live."

"Is that all?"

"That is not all. You must pass along your knowledge of the secret invisibility ray."

When someone tells you it's not gonna hurt, it does, Harry knows. Same with being told you may be allowed to live.

He says, "My ears are ringing from the rough treatment, Fritz, and I'm seeing stars. Can you speak up?"

The first lesson of street fighting was to hit first and hit hard.

Wessel doesn't take the bait but a Luger-toting thug does, stepping closer. Harry miraculously recovers from his befuddlement.

Wrists free of the cord, he jerks his arms up and forward, grabs the closest thug by the lapels, comes off his back foot, and slams his forehead into his nose, hearing the satisfying sound of crushed cartilage, a move he'd perfected on the football field.

As the Kraut drops to his knees, gushing blood and screaming, Harry pivots and buries a toe into the second Luger's groin, with force similar to that of the general's boy at *Kristallnacht*. His Luger goes off, perforating the ceiling as he falls flat on his back, groaning and howling.

Harry pivots again at the Lab Coat and takes his hand. The PVDE types want nothing to do with Harry. Their bribe money won't cover a trip to the hospital.

Lab Coat says, "They have men in the rear who will be coming at the sound of the gunshot, sir. What can we do?"

At the door, he searches in vain for the button and says, "Damned good question."

Outside, there is the sound of spinning tires, the smell of burning rubber.

The door is slammed. It caves inward, smashed by the rear of a car. Its horn honks nonstop.

Harry recognizes the rear bumper and taillights of a 1938 Ford sedan.

Harry and Lab Coat crawl through an opening in the ruined door.

Harry says, "Our taxi is here. Hop in."

CHAPTER 22

Dorothy is driving the 1938 Ford sedan, slamming through the gears like Barney Oldfield, driving fast enough to rattle one's fillings loose on the wooden roadway.

"I could kiss you, Wonder Woman," Harry says.

"Shut up, Antonelli. Must I remind you that when you were a kid, you acted like a smart aleck when you were scared?"

"I'm not complaining, but all the stories have the guy-hero rescuing the damsel in distress, yet I'm the one in distress."

"Think nothing of it. Again."

"How did you home in on me? Your secret powers and those devices in your invisible airplane?"

She laughs. "Did you think we'd trust you outside our rooms by yourself? Oh please, Harry."

"Where's David?"

"We took turns babysitting you, sitting by our doors, ears pressed against them, listening for tomfoolery, losing sleep we desperately need, and this is my shift. I awakened my brother before I went downstairs to see where you and your English friend were going."

"That fake Limey's no friend of mine."

"So I gathered when they carried you into that car. What's this about the tons of gold Peter Owen egged you on with? Are you holding out on us?"

"Not me, I swear. Gold is what I'd like to know too. Where're we going?"

She races under a red light. "I haven't thought that far ahead. Anywhere but where we were."

"Dorothy, out with it. David wouldn't let you do this if you were just a vacationing schoolmarm."

"Yes, I admit that I'm on the government payroll too. On temporary duty."

"Is that the truth?"

"Maybe."

"Hah. I know you don't like to teach girls how to bake cookies and sew buttons on, but this is going overboard. That purse of yours you're never without, do you have your badge in it, it and everything but the kitchen sink?"

"It's none of your business, Antonelli."

"You're on the government payroll as what? It has to do with your science and math background, doesn't it? How it's useful with uranium."

"I can't tell you now."

"Later?"

"No."

"C'mon. Where the hell are we going?" Harry says. "And where'd you come up with this car?"

"We have a rented garage where we keep it. That's our best bet for now."

"So you had a garage rented and waiting for you, huh? To store your major appliances, Frigidaires piled high beside this car?"

"No, please if I may interrupt. Not to your garage if that is where you are bound, miss and sir," says the scientist, who is leaning between them from the back seat. "Please. We must go to the airfield as fast as we can."

"Why?" Dorothy asks.

Speaking fast, the scientist tells all he knows. The radioactive isotope, the evil powder that is now ready, London. All.

"Shit," Harry says. "We have to stop them in their fucking tracks to save the fucking planet, the rotten fuckers."

"Harry, because of our predicament, I'll excuse your toilet mouth."

"And not send me to the principal's office. Good."

"Please, really. We must hurry to the airport," the scientist says. "Since they have been discovered, they have moved their timetable up do this immediately. The Blond Beast ordered it before he was whisked away."

"Who?"

"Reinhard Heydrich. There is a rumor that he was in an accident."

"Him? Yeah, he walked into a door," Harry says.

Dorothy swerves onto a side street and U-turns. "Thanks to your heroism, they're rushing ahead in disarray. We can hope."

"Heroism? I was trying to save my own hide. Either you're a helluva driver, Dorothy, or they're not chasing us."

"I'm not talking to you, Horatio Alger. I'm talking to our passenger."

Feelings hurt, Harry says, "They were going to use us to transport and release the powder, then shove us out of the plane after it was over London."

"I believe this to be true, sir and miss."

"Hey, what is your actual name, Lab Coat? We can't be calling you Mad Scientist," Harry says. "It's impolite."

"Ira Pendleton-Hume."

Harry laughs. "C'mon. No fooling? Shouldn't you be dressed in red, hunting foxes?"

"Harry," Dorothy says.

"That is all right, madame. It is odd, as is my biography. Me, with the face of a Nazi caricature."

"You're adorable," Dorothy says. "Precious."

"Not to the Germans, I am not," Ira Pendleton-Hume says, showing Harry the tattoo on his arm.

"Jesus. Sorry," he says, seeing the numbers. "Not a laughing matter."

"Please do not apologize. My name inspires laughter. That is the common reaction. Even Albert laughed when we were introduced."

"Albert who?"

"Einstein."

"Right. Okay, you're Ira Hyphen from now on."

"That is satisfactory."

The airport is in sight, runway lights on, all else in the area dark. A truck is loading its cargo onto a four-engine transport with engines running, the only activity on the tarmac. The airplane is between a parked one with Italian markings and another with British markings. Where else but Lisbon, Harry thinks, can you find the League of Nations with wings?

"This is an airplane like Hitler's, a Focke-Wulf Condor, but modified," Ira says. "Look on the bottom. The entry door doesn't have built-in steps, probably to save weight. Look at the two cutouts they're closing on the belly. Logically, they've installed a bomb bay.

"The engines are running. They are preparing to take off. That is why they are not chasing after us."

Dorothy says, "What do we do?"

"Since we're in the neighborhood, let's hitch a ride," Harry says. "Gun this jalopy!"

CHAPTER 23

The truck has pulled away, around the corner, out of sight, when Dorothy screeches to a halt 50 yards behind the Condor. The plane's door is being pulled up and closing.

"Shit," Dorothy says. "Goddamnit."

"Dorothy, your mouth," Harry says. "Ira, Mr. Hyphen, pile out and feed them a line."

"Such as what, sir?"

"Uh, you forgot something."

"What could I have forgotten?"

"The second load of uranium poison. The fuse. Your lunch. You'll think of something. Talk isotopes to them. Scoot. Go before they go. *Go!*"

Ira Hyphen does go, scooting the best he can, waving his arms at the airplane.

Harry follows, crouching behind him, then slipping under the airplane.

Ira Hyphen is yelling in yet another language Harry doesn't understand.

An unfriendly Luger-holder new to Harry replies by aiming his weapon at Ira, who covers his face with his hands, a natural reaction, but not a big help unless you're wearing Wonder Woman's magic bracelets.

Taking advantage of the darkness, Harry lunges to the door and pulls on a pair of SS ankles. On an awkward trip to the ground, the

163

Nazi fires at the sky, then lands hard on his ass.

Harry Antonelli, backup placement kicker at the University of Washington, his skill more in demand here than home at the stadium, recalls two misses against Oregon State, both wide to the right. Luckily for him and the team, they won, 26-7.

HISTORICAL NOTE: Harry Antonelli has it wrong again. On October 9, 1937, his Huskies lost to Oregon State, 3-6. Harry wasn't called on to kick.

This time he doesn't miss, drilling a 30-yarder into the Nazi agent's ribs, then uses his writhing body as a stepstool to board. Dorothy is crawling into the airplane behind him, legs dangling. He lifts her on, then Ira Pendleton-Hume.

"You shouldn't be here," Harry yells at her as the engines spool up to full power and they accelerate, tail wheel lifting off the runway.

"I'm Wonder Woman, remember?"

Good point, he thinks as one of the pilots comes out of the cockpit and fires his Luger. The guy has a Mickey Rooney face and a Jack Dempsey physique. There seems to be no shortage of bad guys with Lugers. The bullet kisses Harry's cheek. Another gunshot. The pilot's gun flies out of his hand.

The Lone Ranger and his silver bullets, shooting the guns out of outlaws' hands, Harry thinks, although neither the masked man nor Tonto, his faithful Indian companion, was known for firing a hole through a bandit's hand, drawing blood.

He turns to Dorothy, who's holding a Luger. "I've never fired one of these German things. I was aiming for his head."

"You made a stigmatic out of the no-good—"

"Harry!"

Harry ducks a bloody-fist swing. With an ankle kick and elbow-jerking combination, he pirouettes the pilot out the opened door, listening to his scream fade away as he spirals onto a field adjoining the runway.

"City lights are below, but we're flying cockeyed, at a funny angle," Harry says.

"I'll check on the copilot," Dorothy says, clinging to what she can, seatbacks and bulkheads.

"Sweet-talk him. It's his ass too. Hyphen, are you are all right?"

Ira Pendleton-Hume is greenish, clinging to longitudinal stringers riveted to the bare ceiling.

"I am not so well, but thank goodness they have the powder secured."

Harry looks at the large lead-lined box that's on the floor, jury-rigged with cables and rope directly beside the bomb bay, a crudely-fashioned Dutch door.

"Good, one less problem. Or one more. How do we unload this?"

Ira walks forward, clutching the stringer for support. "A crude arrangement, jury-rigged in haste I'd say. See. The bomb bay is held closed with clamps. Everything's done by hand."

"Meaning one of us doing it with a gun to our heads. Then out we go too."

"Harry," Dorothy screams from the cockpit. "The pilot's dead. Evidently my bullet went through the other's hand to the back of his head."

"Your sights are off," Harry says. "Don't go away."

CHAPTER 24

"Harry, get him the hell out of here," Dorothy says from the copilot's seat as she has them flying straight and level, one hand on the yoke, the other pushing the dead pilot's shoulder away from her.

They're westbound, along the center of the Rio Tejo, heading straight for the Atlantic.

Harry does as she orders, pulling the dead pilot out of the cockpit by his armpits and dumping him on the cabin floor.

He sits down beside her and says, "I'll take it now."

Harry in his comic-strip glory again, Dorothy thinks, sneaking a peek at him.

Terry Lee—ace pilot and star of *Terry and the Pirates*—this time. She admits to herself that she likes the strip too and Terry Lee, a cutie, does remind her of Harry and vice versa. Both handsome and reckless, one fictional and the other—a good question.

Superheroes in the funny papers, however, do not have to exercise restraint and use common sense. Harry has been performing magnificently, but he has limitations, one of which is flying a four-engine German airplane.

"Like hell you will, Harry. How many hours did you have in the baby Piper Cub before you were kicked out of ROTC? That little sixty-five horsepower puddle jumper?"

"Three hundred hours, give or take a few," he says, fudging by only 250.

"Well, I have five hundred hours and advanced ratings, in bigger planes too. Once I co-piloted a DC-3."

Harry looks at the instrument panel; it looks like a dashboard pulled out of 50 cars made into one. Four tachometers, one for each engine. Airspeed indicator, altimeter, rate of climb indicator, compass, and a bunch of other engine-monitoring dials like oil pressure that are in German, all Greek to him.

"I can fly it by the seat of my pants."

"Harry, you can crash us by the seat of your pants without even trying."

This is a rare instance when Harry knows it's time to give in. "Okay, okay. Take it."

She squeezes his forearm. "Stop pouting like an infant. You can help me. These levers between us are the throttles."

"I know what they are."

"There's a tremendous vibration as we pick up speed. The landing gear must still be down and I can't find the lever by feel."

Harry looks around the center console. "This wheel-shaped thing?"

"Try it."

The landing gear comes up with a hydraulic hum and a clunk.

"That's better. There's still a terrible vibration. The passenger door, is it open?"

Harry twists around. "I think it sheared off."

"You're bleeding," Dorothy says.

"A flesh wound. I hope."

"Sir!" Ira Pendleton-Hume screams.

The pilot she killed has returned from the dead, lunging into the cockpit, swinging wildly.

The bullet was apparently deflected by the partition, a glancing flesh wound that knocked him cold, Harry thinks. He shoves backward out of his seat, taking the resurrected pilot along as the pilot pummels him. The guy doesn't look exactly like Boris Karloff, but is behaving like a pissed-off Frankenstein.

Harry pummels him in return, neither doing much damage, like punch-drunk boxers working on each other's cauliflower ears. Flailing away, they fall and roll on the floor as the plane pitches and yaws.

The pilot gets a lucky roll, caroming Harry off the uranium box.

He regains his feet and gives Harry a hard boot to his back, shoving him toward the door opening, where he's sucked out the opening by the kick and the slipstream.

He grabs onto the floor lip that surrounds the absent door with one hand and then the other, hanging at an angle by his fingers.

The pilot is right there, lifting a foot to stomp on Harry's fingertips.

"Ow!"

Ira Hyphen has buried his teeth in the ankle of the pilot's other leg.

Harry is able to grab the pilot's calf and hoist himself aboard, then lifting it, sending the pilot to the floor, flat on his back.

Ira jumps onto the pilot's midsection, knocking the wind out of him.

He collaborates with Harry to lift his shoulders and send him into free fall, a nicely-executed swan dive.

"Thanks, Ira Hyphen. I owe you."

"Not a fraction as much as I owe you, sir."

They look at their cargo. "Any ideas what to do with this deadly shit?"

"The uranium isotope is U- two-thirty—"

"I know all that. How do we jettison it?"

"I have a confession to make," Ira says.

"It can wait. The middle of the Atlantic is three or four miles deep. Can we steer it out that way? The worst it can do is poison some sharks."

"Yes we can, I believe."

"I'll buy that, but what about us?"

"Parachutes. Shall we look?"

Harry hears popcorn popping. Not so. Bullets are piercing the fuselage.

"Harry!" Dorothy yells. "We have company."

"Buckle up," he tells Ira as he guides him into a jump seat.

CHAPTER 25

Harry assumes his cockpit seat in time to see a fighter plane streak by on their starboard side.

"It's a Messerschmitt Bf-109," Dorothy says. "With no swastika or any other markings. It's the best German fighter."

"You're sure?"

"I am. David and I took a class in aircraft recognition. See the flat-glass canopy? Water-cooled engine. Inverted V-12, liquid-cooled, fuel-injected. Being fuel-injected rather than fed by a carburetor, the 109 can fly upside down without loss of power. It'll do over 350 miles per hour, twice as fast as this tub, and it has guns, we don't."

Strangely, Harry is less frightened by large, rapid-fire guns blasting at them from a distance than he is of a Luger pointed at him from a yard away, firepower 50 times as lethal.

"You and Dave get an A. They must store the thing in a hangar in neutral Lisbon. Or it flew over from neutral Spain next door," Harry says as he watches it swing around behind them. "We're neutral sitting ducks."

"Harry, should I dive or climb?"

"Straight up or straight down, it can outfly us and it's armed."

"That's not a constructive answer."

Harry squints ahead. He sees a large aircraft that is illuminated by a full moon.

"Hey, look, the Pan Am Clipper is coming in from the Azores. The one you rode into town on. Head toward it."

"And crash into it instead of being shot to pieces, Harry? Some choice."

"Lemme take the controls. We'll fly under it."

She slaps his hand. "Leave the yoke alone. Wonderful idea, but I'll do the honors."

Dorothy goes into a shallow dive, advances the throttles to full power, and banks northbound, G-forces making their cheeks droop. Vibration and turbulence intensify.

A terrified Ira Pendleton-Hume has entered the cockpit. Gripping their seat backs, he says, "Are we going to die?"

Harry doesn't answer his question. "Dorothy, this will be exactly like flying under a bridge. When flying under a bridge, never look up at the bridge or you'll smash into it."

"Harry, please shut up."

She will take his advice, though, as he undoubtedly speaks from experience.

Harry says, looking out, "The Kraut fighter's right on our ass again."

Dorothy has leveled out, banking hard southbound. She crosses under the Clipper at right angles, an instantaneous lunar eclipse.

The Messerschmidt-109 peels off just behind the Clipper, as Dorothy crosses under. Both planes are so low that they raise waves in the river.

The Messerschmitt hasn't quite leveled out. It catches a wingtip in the water and goes end-over-end, breaking into pieces.

"Okay, good, great, beautiful," Harry says, kissing her cheek. "But let's amscray before his friends come."

"To where, Harry? We haven't had time to think this out."

She fumbles around the instrument panel and says, "Do we have an autopilot?"

"What's that?"

"An automatic pilot is a contraption that flies the plane without a pilot. By a pneumatically-spun gyroscopic effect that operates the controls. So I was told in flight training. I'm not seeing any levers or dials for one."

"That's swell for the plane, but what about us?"

"Parachutes?"

"The pilots were wearing them."

"Oh."

"'Oh' is right, Harry."

But for the drone of the engines, as they leave Portugal behind, there is silence until Ira says, "Please head back toward Lisbon. I will search everywhere for extra parachutes."

CHAPTER 26

As Dorothy gains altitude and brings the plane around over the Rio Tejo, Ira holds up two parachutes and says, "These are spares in the storage locker. Just these two. For you, sir and miss, when we get in position. You can float into the water without harm."

"And you're gonna jump out and flap your wings?"

"I am doomed," he says, unbuttoning his shirt to show chest sores. "I was exposed to radiation. They made me do much of the work in the transfer of the isotope. To save my family, they said. If they were lying, there was nothing I could do anyway. Show me how to work the controls and I will point the plane into the ocean until it runs out of fuel. Who knows, maybe I will land softly and it will float. I can have another week or two to live."

"Looks like chicken pox," Harry says. "Don't worry. Everyone gets it."

"No, Ira," Dorothy says. "You are not going down with this ship."

"I second the motion, Hyphen," Harry says.

Ira says, "But sir and miss, I searched everyplace. I fear there are two and only two chutes."

"Okay, this is what we'll do," Harry says. "Dorothy, can you make one of those pneumonia autopilot things by tying the seatbelts around the controls and aim it toward the ocean? We're close enough to open water that we can't miss."

"I'll try," she says.

"We'll strap on the chutes, and fly low and slow, and I'll jump out

173

over the river with Ira. It'll be a soft landing. We'll swim ashore."

"Harry, you don't know how to swim. I thought you were afraid of water too."

"Hey, I'm afraid of guns and clowns, not water."

"Aha! Clowns," Dorothy yells. "I knew it. I knew it, I knew it. I just knew it."

A death-bed kind of confession, Harry thinks; not much is going my way today.

"I insist, ma'am and sir. Turn around and after you show me how to work the controls, I will fly the plane into the middle of the ocean and angle it downward after it runs out of gas."

"Wait a minute, not so fast," Harry says. "Do you know how to fix your mad science lab so it can't make any more of this powder or anything else, ever."

"Yes I do."

"Does anybody else?"

"No, not as well as I. Nobody who would cooperate. They are Germans or people owned by the Germans."

"Do you know where it is, the building?"

"No. We were moved blindfolded from the airport and confined to the facility."

"Other than passing onto a wharf to get to it and thumping along on heavy timbers, me neither."

"My confession, sir."

"Oh yeah. Is it important and do we have time for it? We're kind of busy now, Ira."

"The powder does not work as the Germans demand that it will. It is too, shall we say, dilute. It was impossible with our small centrifuge and our knowledge of nuclear fission to make the isotope do what the Germans think it will do. If the powder drops on London, it will be so scattered and diffused, it will not be too harmful. That is how I stayed alive. We are carrying one ton of slightly-enriched uranium. I calculate that it would require an aerial armada carrying eight thousand tons of it to be effective."

Dorothy says, "There aren't that many airplanes available. Hitler would have to borrow some from Churchill and FDR."

"An apt comparison," Ira says.

"Shit. So I'm not saving the fucking world?"

"But you are, sir. I suspect that the Germans will retry on their own and waste many frustrating years. You are instrumental in giving them false expectations that will divert many of their research resources. There is also the possibility they will succeed, which will be horrendously hideous for the world."

"Who's the guy who escaped and died that horrible death?"

"My brother," Ira says. "In the process of development, he was the lead scientist. There were accidents. He lived with the material day after day, contaminating himself. The powder *is* deadly, but not mass-murder deadly. My brother knew he was a dead man anyway if they discovered that the project was a failure and by doing so, perpetuated the myth that we were making a deadly weapon. He practically bathed in it, coating himself when the Nazi minders were not looking."

"So it's your brother who saved the world?" Harry says.

"You can share the credit, sir. You deserve to."

"Yeah, well."

Dorothy has the plane in position, headed east on the Tejo, close to the north shore and Lisbon.

"Can you boys put an end to your coffee klatch," Dorothy says, getting up and putting on her chute. "The Clipper has just touched down. We can go."

"Keep your lips buttoned on this, okay?" Harry tells Ira.

"Yes sir."

Harry looks downward, unsure of the wisdom of jumping out of a perfectly good airplane.

"Go," Harry yells to her.

She jumps out the doorway, hands clasped to her chest.

Like she's done it before, Harry thinks. *In her top-secret secret agent training.*

He throws his arms around Ira.

"We cannot do this, sir. I will fly the plane to the Atlantic."

"Bullshit you will. It'll fly itself. How much do you weigh?"

"Sixty kilos."

"I'm not thinking straight. How much is one kilo?"

"One kilogram."

"Right. Don't tell me how much that is in English. You're as light as a feather."

"Very well, but we must hurry."

Harry squeezes him tighter and says, "Ira Hyphen, old pal, don't get any funny ideas that we're going steady."

Out they go, Harry envying Superman, who can defenestrate an airplane without a chute.

CHAPTER 27

As the Condor wobbles out to sea, both chutes open with a pop and a jerk, Dorothy's 100 feet lower.

Harry partially loses his grip on Ira, but hangs on with one hand. "Can you see what looks like your uranium building, Ira?"

"Over there, by the water, toward downtown, those three warehouses joined together. By the elongated shape of the structure, I am certain. It has to be the one."

Harry fumbles with the Minox, aims, says, "Say cheese," and clicks the shutter.

"I'd take another, but I'd need my other hand to advance the film."

"One, yes sir, one photograph is fine."

Due to their additional heft, Harry plus 60 kilos (132 pounds), they float by Dorothy, who blows them a kiss as they drift downward.

Dorothy, the secret paratrooper.

If they survive the night, they'll have to have a chitchat about her duties other than as a schoolmarm.

"Sir!" Ira screams, waving his free arm.

Another Messerschmitt Bf-109 is racing toward them from the west, straight and level, guns blazing, bullets zinging by them.

"Duck," he tells Ira.

"Duck where, sir?"

Damn good question. Before Harry ducks, he looks up at Dorothy. She has taken from her purse an automatic pistol that dwarfs her hand. Maybe an American service-model Colt .45.

She is firing, not aiming, simply emptying the gun ahead of the German fighter. Harry is thinking she's panicking; he can hardly blame her.

The Messerschmitt flies between them, a deafening hurricane blowing Harry and Ira sideways. As they recover to the vertical, the Nazi fighter flattens out above the water and lands on it as if it were the Clipper, despite doing 300 miles per hour and not being a seaplane. It vanishes in an erupting froth of water and aluminum.

Just ahead of Dorothy, Harry and Ira land on the lower portion of the Tower of Belém, which Harry regards fondly as an asymmetrical wedding cake. Built as a fortress from 1514–1520, it was the starting point of explorers who set out to discover the trade routes. A tourist attraction now, it still has a practical use, he thinks.

Harry runs underneath Dorothy, catching her, breaking her fall.

Holding her as they collapse together, he says, "When did you become such a deadeye?"

"It was child's play. I fired ahead of him and let him fly into my bullets. One lucky bullet was all that was required to do the job. Hitting the pilot or a vital part of the engine."

Her chute falls to the ground, covering them.

"Harry, don't," she says.

They are across from Salazar's World Exhibition, the *Esposição do Mundo Português*. Everyone is clapping their hands, thinking it's all part of the extravaganza.

Free of Harry's embrace, Dorothy lifts the silk and they come out from under it. They blow kisses to the cheering onlookers and walk to the sidewalk. A parachute stunt and downed airplanes; he'd applaud too.

"If we had a wrist radio like Dick Tracy's, we could call your brother."

"There is no such thing and there never will be, but there is such a thing as a phone booth, Horatio Alger."

They go to the first one they spot.

David Booth turns up in 10 minutes in a 1937 Ford.

"You sell cars along with major appliances, Dave? Buicks and Fords?" Harry says, in the car, giving him the Minox and relating Ira's story fast.

"One more thing, Harry, sir," Ira says in the car. "Are you familiar with Reinhard Heydrich?"

"By golly, I am. Now that you mention it, we have met. Informally."

"He flew in from Berlin and visited, terrifying us."

"Really?" Harry says.

"The man is a beast, a monster. He is ordering more powder, on a faster deadline, on a crash program basis. Hitler and Himmler approved. If this was meant for London, the next batch is earmarked for the United States."

Harry smiles. "Reinhard and I discussed that among other stuff."

Dorothy says, "Ira, honey, be truthful, are you really dying or not?"

"No, no. The sores. I have many allergies. I was very careful as I know more than anyone the power of this terrible material in large dosages."

Dorothy says, "The Germans are holding your family hostage in the camps?"

He shakes his head. "Friends *and* relatives. Even neighbors who we only knew in passing, in saying hello at the grocer's, like that. The Nazis are thorough at every diabolical thing they do. At least a hundred people I know of. I know they're already dead. The last letters they sent said all was well. I know they were forced to."

"How?"

"How they wrote, the phrasing. Speaking of hometowns that weren't ours and cousins who did not exist. That stopped. They must have been found out. Now the letters are forgeries. Good forgeries, but forgeries just the same. Then they stopped altogether."

"I am so sorry about your brother and the rest of your family," Dorothy says.

Ira begins crying. "He sacrificed himself so that the world could know."

"Driver, I'll double your fare if you step on the gas," Harry tells David, who has been uncharacteristically silent.

CHAPTER 28

Things are happening too damn fast for Harry Antonelli and too damn slowly. He has a jackhammering headache, which he knows will get worse and he also knows that he isn't done being knocked on the noggin, him being who he is.

David zeroes right in on another pay telephone by a cigarette shop and makes several calls, the numbers all from memory.

Hmm, Harry thinks.

They wait at a photo store David knows the directions to (by memory), while the film is processed—a store whose owner just happens to have gotten out of bed and is waiting, right on the job, an eager beaver. This is a Portuguese photo-store guy who David called—David—who doesn't speak Portuguese... as far as Harry knows.

Make that a double *hmm*.

After he and Ira go over the prints with the shop owner, David borrows the photographer's phone and makes another call. David's eyes alone tell Harry and the others that it's a private call (or two?) and to stay the hell out of the way. Harry doesn't think he's phoning anyone in the major appliance business.

They drive right to the uranium plant, *thump-thump-thump* and all. An army unit David says the Embassy trusts is already there with trucks, swarming into the Nazi uranium plant.

Ira goes inside to supervise and identify Nazis, who on his word are being taken out in handcuffs. Innocents are separated, taken out, but not in cuffs.

Except Horst Wessel, Harry notices.

Or Peter Owen.

Chickens who've flown the coop.

"What's next, chief?" Harry asks David.

"I have no further work to do in Lisbon," David tells Harry. "I am not officially here and we are catching the Clipper out in the morning."

"What about the stoves and washing machines on order?" Harry says.

David stares at him. "I will never comprehend your sense of humor."

"Dorothy, you're leaving too?" Harry says.

She says, "Sorry, Harry. We're done babysitting. You're on your own."

David says, "I've been advised that the Clipper is departing earlier than the normal schedule. The incidents with low-flying German aircraft has understandably made Pan Am nervous."

"I don't blame them," Harry says. "An international incident if I ever saw one."

"Yes. It seems there was an incident of near misses with two low-flying, high-performance aircraft. Two fatal crashes."

"Not part of the exhibition entertainment program?" Harry says.

David smiles at him.

Harry says, "I will never comprehend your sense of humor."

Davis laughs.

"Yeah," Harry says. "Flying is risky business in this day and age with all the horsepower and unbelievable speeds."

Dorothy takes Harry's arm. "Enough banalities, you two. You can buy me a farewell drink downtown."

Harry is making plans for what will be next after five or six farewell drinks when he hears a sneeze.

Horst Wessel has slipped out a side door. He's in the tan Buick, speeding away.

"Can I borrow the car tonight, Dad?" Harry says to David as he gets behind the wheel of the Ford before receiving an answer, a protest either verbal or physical, and lays a remarkable amount of rubber.

CHAPTER 29

If driving in Lisbon is dangerous during the day, Harry thinks, it's ab-so-lute-ly lethal at night. Forget traffic lights. The only lights obeyed are oncoming headlights.

He figures that he knows the city as well or better than Horst Wessel. The Nazi loses him at intersections where everyone has the green light, even if they don't, and over the crests of roller-coaster hills too, but Harry is able to reconnect via parallel streets. There is just enough illumination from shops and cafés to keep him alive.

The chase ends at the foot of Castelo de São Jorge. It's closed for the day. Not that it has attracted many tourists lately. Hitler's throttled tourism everywhere in Europe and the majority of those in Lisbon are at Belém, at Salazar's expensive county fair. Harry and Wessel have the castle to themselves.

Wessel is carrying something up a concrete ramp that leads into the castle.

"What's the hurry, Hans?" Harry yells, getting out of the Ford. "We have unfinished business, you and I."

A bullet pings against a fender, another blows out the driver's section of windshield glass.

"You're loony as a shithouse rat, Wessel. Your head's on crooked. Give it up. You and your uranium game, it's over. The final whistle has blown and you're a four-touchdown loser."

Wessel's third bullet whizzes above Harry's head. He doesn't know how many rounds a Luger or any other real-life pistol holds,

184

so he doesn't keep count, prudently thinking that it holds one more than the last shot.

The Lone Ranger and all the other Hollywood cowboys have six-shooters that hold at least 20 bullets. Not a comforting thought.

Wessel sneezes and says, "It is not over, Antonelli. The *Führer* has given his blessing. We will restart elsewhere."

"Your Berlin boss is nuttier than a fucking fruitcake, Wessel. The game's over in Lisbon."

Two shots, so wild that Harry doesn't see or hear what they hit. He follows Wessel inside the castle walls. Safely (so he hopes) behind a pillar of centuries-old stone, he yells, "Hitler was gassed in the Great War. It's still in his head. Him and his plan to take over the world—"

This shot creases Harry's shirt sleeve and forearm. It feels like a row of bee stings.

"Quit interrupting me, asshole. A guy named Santayana was quoted as saying, 'Those who do not remember the past are doomed to repeat it.' Hitler should have it tattooed on his eyelids."

"Our *Führer* is the messiah, the savior of the Nordic race. The greatest leader in the history of mankind, and I once sat next to him. This is a minor setback. Spare me your gibberish."

"Son of a bitch," Harry says. "Adolf was in town, wasn't he, checking out your crazy project?"

Wessel doesn't answer. He goes inside a crenulated tower and to a parapet on the top. He faces the Rio Tejo and blinks the mystery object he's carrying, a flashlight.

Harry says from around a corner, "What's that, Fritz, a secret code? Flash Gordon used one too."

"I have an escape plan. I will descend after the return signal, finish you off, walk through Alfama, and catch a Brazilian freighter. Ah, there it is, the return signal."

"Wishful thinking. They're not tooting their horn for you, and even if they were, you're a mile away with me between you and them."

"You know nothing."

"Even if you're goofy wish comes true, they won't be giving you a ride out of the goodness of their hearts. Let me guess what they want from you. Gold."

That earns Harry a harmless bullet that raises sparks against a wall.

"You demanded gold from me that I didn't have, Herr Wessel."

"Gold to finance the salvation of Aryan civilization, you fool."

"A cause as worthy as clogging sewers. Are you convinced, finally, at long last, that I'm not King Midas?"

Harry sidearms the ingot he'd found at Peter's. It lands with a melodious ring at Wessel's feet.

Harry charges upward as Wessel bends down for it, planning to snag the Luger. He doesn't account for the flashlight.

Wessel clobbers him on the side of the head. Batteries go flying and Harry's head clobbers the other side of the parapet wall.

Up comes the Luger. Its barrel is as large as the battlements' cannons. Harry is on the verge of throwing up.

"You're out of shells, Wessel," he says. "I kept count."

"So did I," Wessel says, laughing. "I can spare you a few seconds to say your prayers."

"Tell you what, I'll pray that your gun's empty while you pray that you can find the gold without me."

Wessel moistens his lips and his hand wavers. Harry pushes off the wall and at him.

Bang.

The shot makes Harry's ears ring.

Click.

Music to his ears.

Wessel sneezes, buying Harry a priceless second as Wessel tries to change clips.

"Gesundheit, fuckhead," Harry says, slamming into him, sending the pistol flying.

They trade blows, mostly deflected by forearms and elbows. Harry catches Wessel by surprise by stepping back, then plunging forward.

He knees him in the gut, slams him against the wall, and picks up the ingot. "Will this be enough for your steamship ticket?"

Holding his midsection, Wessel says, "Give it to me."

They hear a ship's horn.

Harry lobs the ingot onto a ledge. "They're not gonna wait all night."

Wessel lunges for it.

Harry dives as if for a fumbled football, catches Wessel as he's bent forward, off balance, lifts him by the ankles, and holds him over the ledge.

"Hey, Wessel, I'll pull you up if you tell me what your real moniker is, before you had it changed."

"Is that a promise?"

"Scout's honor."

"Does that mean the truth, a promise?"

"I swear on a stack of Bibles that it's the honest-to-God truth."

"Fritz Hansnegle."

"Really?"

"It is. Do as you vowed and pull me up."

Harry releases him.

And listens to a fading German obscenity.

CHAPTER 30

Harry drives without benefit of a windshield to the Hotel Metropole. He can't see worth a damn, which makes the traffic slightly less terrifying and the breeze is refreshing.

In the Booth suite, Dorothy cleans up his face and arm.

"You look like the Brooklyn Dodgers used you for batting practice," an amused David says, watching from the bathroom doorway, arms folded.

"Thanks for the sympathy, Dave."

"You aren't going to tell us what happened after you stole my car?"

"Borrowed, not stole. I don't want you kids being accessories before or after the fact."

"I dread asking what condition it is in now."

"Perfect. Like right out of the showroom. Ouch, goddamnit!"

Dorothy says, dabbing his arm, "Stop whining, you big baby. Iodine will kill the germs. I can't do a thing for the lump on the side of your head."

"I walked into a door."

"Before or after which fact?" David says.

"I flubbed the words. I just went out for a spin on a nice evening."

"Did you cross paths with that horrid Nazi you dunked?" Dorothy says.

"Him? Nah. He oughta be hightailing in to Berlin so he can get in an iron lung before his cold turns into pneumonia."

"Why did you steal the car then? We thought you did it to pursue him."

"I was, but he lost me after the third corner. The engine in that car must be souped up."

"You said you didn't cross paths with him," Dorothy says. "I take that to mean you didn't see him."

"Semantics," Harry says. "You're trying to put words in my mouth."

"You remind me of your cat," David says.

"Hey, thanks, Dave. That's the nicest thing you've ever said to me."

David gazes at the ceiling for guidance, finds none, and goes into his room.

After Dorothy completes her first aid, Harry reaches for her, saying that he wants to duplicate what Ira and him were doing in midair.

"Not so fast, Romeo."

She goes to her purse and gives him a picture postcard of Castelo de São Jorge.

"They sell these all over town. It's a popular Lisbon landmark," she says.

He looks at her. "Why that castle? What's this mean?"

"What do you mean, *what does this mean*, Harry? Your eyes are as big as saucers."

Harry will never ever tell her what he's done with Fritz Hansnegle/ Horst Wessel. The bastard was a Nazi fanatic and a cold-blooded killer, yeah, but Dorothy might not appreciate Harry as a murderer too, along with his other perceived faults, lying to the German in the process. It may be okay for her Spitfire ace to ventilate Nazis in midair, but not for him to drop one into midair. Dames could be funny.

"Nothing."

"Nothing?"

Harry shrugs.

Dorothy sighs.

"David didn't give you the third degree about your latest scrapes and bruises. He knew it'd be hopeless. I do too."

Harry shrugs.

Dorothy gives him a pen and says, "While I change into something more comfortable, you *are* to write on this postcard to your parents. I'll deliver it after we're home. You will be tested when I return from changing clothes. If you fail the test, you sleep in the parlor again."

Feeling enormous pressure, a guilty Harry sits down and begins *Dearest Mother and Father, I know I've been the rottenest son...*

He's still there white knuckling his pencil, when Dorothy comes out in something more comfortable, pink and gauzy. She looks over his shoulder.

"I can't help it. I have writer's block, like I did when I had a term paper due."

"Stop right there, tear up the postcard and try the next one. That is not you, Antonelli. Your mother will eat it up, but your father will see through you in a second."

Harry tosses his pencil aside.

"Write or I'll change into something less comfortable, especially my girdle that's armor-plated."

Harry retrieves the pencil and stares at a duplicate postcard.

Dear Mom and Dad,

Having a wonderful time (sometimes), wish you were here only when I am. It's crazy in Europe, and sometimes I could use Tabby as a bodyguard. I hope to be home to see you soon.

With much love,

Harry

"That's my boy."

"Yeah," he says, wiping his eyes.

Dorothy sits on dewy-eyed Harry's lap.

She strokes his forehead and says, "It's short, by no means *War and Peace*, but it's you. Congratulations. You passed."

"Does your Spitfire pilot write his parents?"

"He has no living parents."

"Jeez. I'm sorry," Harry says.

"You don't have to pretend to be sorry."

"Okay, I won't."

"My dashing Spitfire ace has no parents because he doesn't exist."

"Huh?" Harry says. "Hah!"

"I made you jealous, didn't I?"

"And you gave me an inferiority complex too."

"Can we talk for a minute, Harry?"

Uh oh. "Sure. I'm all ears."

"They call them phobias, you know."

Playing dumb, he says, "I don't know what you mean."

"I can understand guns. Anyone with half a brain is afraid of guns."

Harry knows where this is going. "Can we please drop it?"

"Were you molested by a clown when you were a tiny child?"

"Jesus Christ. No. Well, I don't think so."

By now, after all these years, Dorothy thinks she knows when Harry is lying, and it isn't now.

"Please calm down. When I was little, I was terrified by people on crutches. Once I saw a character in a comic book on crutches and went into hysterics. That's what I mean by a phobia. I had one too. Phobias aren't to be ashamed of."

"Are you still afraid of them?"

"Just when I pass somebody close on the sidewalk."

He reaches for her, saying, "Phobias. Something we have in common."

Just as they kiss, David's door opens, then slams shut. Hard.

David goes to the fridge for a bottle of soda, takes it into his room, and slams it shut. Hard.

Knowing that they have a determined chaperone, Dorothy sighs and gets up. She gives Harry a forehead peck.

"Tomorrow morning is coming early and I have to pack."

"Have you thought of saving a seat for Ira Hyphen on the Clipper? It'd be swell if he can amscray out of this town."

"He's waiting in line at the dock. We wanted to be sure he'd get on."

"He has a ticket?"

David opens his door and says, "He does."

Dorothy smiles, goes to her door, and blows Harry a kiss.

After she closes and locks her door, Harry says to her brother, "Come here and dump out that sugary stuff. It's bad for your teeth. Your dad would tell you that. Have a beer with me. You're second fiddle, but you're all the company I have. And I don't like to drink alone unless I'm alone."

"Certainly," David says after hesitating.

David brings out a Super Bock for Harry and for himself.

They toast and David says, "You did all we asked and then some, Harry."

"Do I get a medal?"

"You don't."

"Why not?"

"The project, me, the Nazis, the deadly uranium isotope, the highly-satisfactory denouement, the local collaborators, none of it occurred. Officially."

"Okay, no medal. Fine. Do I get more money?"

"No. Your mission is over."

"Gold?"

David smiles.

"What the hell does that Mona Lisa smile mean?"

"I'll merely say that Dorothy's science and metallurgy background has been extraordinarily useful."

"Okay, let's move along from your cryptic bullshit, Dave. Tell me something."

David Booth tenses. "What?"

"Do you have a gal back home?"

"I'm too busy. It wouldn't be fair to her."

"Busy working for your secret agency, huh? Yours and your sis's?"

"Which will remain confidential. Give it up, Harry."

"Does your secret agency have a secret handshake?"

David closes his eyes.

"You're awfully jittery, you know."

"Don't worry about me, Harry."

"You know, the night's still young and if you don't have a steady gal, I can arrange for a taxi to take you where you need to go. A ten-minute trip to a part of town where nobody knows nobody."

"That's inappropriate, Harry."

"I know. And fun too. So I've heard."

"Harry, may I speak frankly?"

"If I say no?"

"Dorothy is not and never was boy crazy."

"I know. It's just one of her many great qualities."

"There are times that I regret she isn't," David says after a long pull of Super Bock. "Good night, Harry."

"Good night, Dave."

"Oh, one other thing, Harry," he says at his door. "The Minox."

"What about it?"

"It's government property, not an item to be sold at a pawn shop. Hand it over."

Harry digs it out of a pocket and hands it over, wondering if mind reading is taught in top-secret spy school.

With nothing better or worse to do, Harry drinks himself silly and falls asleep, wondering about Dave. About Dorothy. About Maria Fernanda. About Countess Magda. About Wonder Woman flying her invisible airplane off the comic strip and landing in front of him.

When he awakens in the morning, the Booth siblings are gone.

He had slept through Dorothy kissing a fingertip and touching Harry's cheek ever so gently.

That or he dreamt she did.

CHAPTER 31

In the morning, his head pounding, Harry heads out to find and butt antlers with Peter Owen, for a pound of flesh and/or an ingot or two or five of gold. He's running low on cash and there's nothing on the horizon, a hustle or a secret agent fee. Nothing.

It occurs to him that he hadn't asked David if in his secret organization there's a secret pay scale for saving the world, whether he flopped at it or not, and if Dorothy and Ira get credit for doing most of the dirty work. He knows that somehow he's been screwed, as he had with the wine corks.

Harry picks Peter's lock with Dorothy's bobby pin (which he will keep for sentimental reasons) and discovers Peter tucked neatly into what remains of his bed, covered by his least-dirty sheet. But for the bullet hole in his forehead and a Nazi gold ingot wedged in his mouth, he appears to be sleeping peacefully, eyes closed and, for once, lips sealed. A pillow with two holes in it is on the floor, a make-do silencer. As if anyone in this neighborhood hasn't heard gunfire or cares to investigate if they do.

Harry opens the closet and finds the bookshop Nazi-sissy Dieter there, in the same state of health, one difference being he's vertical instead of horizontal, rigor mortis enabling him to lean against the wall like an ironing board. The second difference being paper wadded inside his mouth rather than gold. Inside his shirt, he's stuffed with paper too, giving him the appearance of being blown up by a tire pump.

Harry removes some of the papers. They're meticulously hand-written in German with page numbers. One appears to be the title page. *Göttdämmerung of Glory.*

Strange. He tosses the paper aside.

Bookshop Dieter—An errand boy sent to retrieve gold, who maybe tried to cut himself a slice of the pie. That's how the Nazis fire people who are insubordinate and don't get the job done right. Keeps the unemployment lines short. Keeps them off the dole.

Harry tries to muster guilt for the poor bastards, but fails. Anybody who resembles Heinrich Himmler and is proud of it, and memorizes *Mein Kampf* like it's the *Magna Carta*—sorry. And Peter too, who led Harry into a trap to be killed, and trailed bullshit behind him like carnival streamers—sorry.

He feels under the floorboards and pulls out 10 more ingots, though no Scotch. Why had they been overlooked?

For a fleeting moment, Harry thinks he's finally arrived at the end of the rainbow.

But no. Something smells fishy, Peter Owen-fishy, fishier than an entire fish market. Every fish in the Rio Tejo.

This gold ignored, the ingot in Peter's mouth, all used in this slaughterhouse like a base metal?

He's remembering Dorothy's words—Dorothy, the science major. And last night, her brother's—him, the ultra-secret agent.

Tungsten is ultra heavy, the same specific gravity as gold. Counterfeiting the English pound, blockading them. The Nazis are cunning monsters. They're capable of anything."

And: *I'll merely say that Dorothy's science and metallurgy background has been extraordinarily useful.*

Harry studies the ingots for similarities other than the dazzling yellow color. Leaving a gold ingot on a stiff is nonsense. Applesauce.

The similarity is the serial numbers. As similar as they can get. They're all are the same, on all 12 of them.

Shit.

He paws through Peter's belongings and finds a nail file. He files an edge of a gold ingot until silver shows through.

He does another ingot. The same.

Shit.

Double shit.

Shit to the power of ten, of a thousand, of a fucking trillion! Gold-plated tungsten. Each and every one of them. The deadliest fool's gold.

The Nazis are buying wolframite with counterfeit gold, smelting it into tungsten, then sending gold-plated tungsten back to Portugal as payment, and financing their doomsday operation with it too. Most likely pocketing the Swiss gold.

He has a final look at Peter Owen, late of Keokuk, Iowa. Or wherever.

Are his killers leaving him and his fakery here as a message?

Bunco artist extraordinaire, Peter was playing three-card monte with one small revision to the game. The gold coming back to Portugal to finance a pyramid of things including a certain uranium isotope was ersatz. Harry remembers the Fourth of July, Independence Day at the Canção, Peter speaking of acquiring slate so that the phantom corks inside the crates would be as heavy as the "olive oil" stamped on the outside of the crates.

Gold-plated tungsten is heavier than corks and bottles too.

Peter was cheating the cheating Germans. He was double- and triple-dealing, and paid for it. Whoever killed him and Dieter— irrelevant. Hired PVDE thugs or freelance gunslingers or actual Krauts, what difference does it make if you're dead?

Where does Maria Fernanda fit in?

He does and doesn't want to know.

Among Horst Wessel/Fritz Hansnegle's last words—*the Brazilian freighter*. Was it a diversionary tactic or for real?

You can't trust anybody these days, Harry thinks.

A whodunit that has to be solved?

But not by him.

Once in great while, Harry can take a hint.

He closes Peter's door quietly behind him.

CHAPTER 32

When Harry isn't moping around town, wishing he had eyes in the back of his head, or in the Hotel Metropole suite (he has learned that it's paid for until the end of the month), whispering to the concealed microphone about the ultra-secret invisibility ray, he's in the Canção, drinking too much, depleting his kitty even further.

Portuguese-English dictionary in hand, he's been scanning the local papers in search of a double *assassinio* of a prominent bookstore manager and a British (?) resident. Also, a tragic *acidente*, the fatal fall from Castelo de São Jorge of the German SS attaché.

Nary a printed word. He presumes the victims have been hauled off to be buried at sea and swept under an official or unofficial rug.

Maria Fernanda Ramos hasn't been in the Canção and the Hitler poster hasn't been replaced, bad news and good. Late one afternoon, on the eighth day of his vigil, she comes in and sits down next to him.

Without preamble she says, "I am so grateful to you for the rescue from the monster Heydrich."

"Happy to do it. Where've you been? It's been days and the manager is worried sick too."

"I've been, oh, where I am safe."

"I've worried the Nazis found you again," he says.

She squeezes his hands. "I am safe."

"My humble home will be safer."

"You have dirty thoughts on your mind," she says, smiling.

"Yes, yes I do," he says, smiling.

198

"I live with an aunt on an edge of Lisbon that foreigners never visit. I have been living there for many months, since the war started."

Why is she revealing this now, he wonders?

"A wise idea. I guess."

"Would you like to see it?"

Harry responds by rushing her out of her seat, out the door, and into a taxi he leaps in front of to hail.

"You could have finished your drink, Harry."

"And you could've changed your mind. Ladies are noted for that."

Maria Fernanda gives the driver directions in rapid-fire Portuguese. She doesn't respond when Harry asks where they're going.

Arms folded tightly, she doesn't respond to anything Harry says.

He looks out his window, pretending to enjoy the scenery, which fast becomes shockingly poor.

It's a 20-minute ride to a northwest section of Lisbon that's semi-rural and scrubby. Donkeys pack cans of olive oil and vinegar, pulling plows too. Burros outnumber cars and trucks.

Maria Fernanda has the driver make multiple turns, as if making it impossible for Harry to find her destination again.

They're off pavement and the roads are rutted, full of potholes, impassable in heavy rain. Houses are becoming few and far between, some not much more than huts. All this shocks Harry, who has never ventured out of downtown Lisbon and the riverfront.

They pull up to a house that's old but large, a faded country estate of stucco, with uneven architecture, add-ons over the years. The landscaping is weedy and overgrown.

Maria Fernanda leads him into a living room containing old chairs, then pushes open a false wall. It's a living room and a half, full of people.

Most refuse eye contact with Harry except one older woman wearing an apron, who appraises him as she dries a plate over and over again, not liking what she sees, probably the aunt. Relatives of Harry's lady friends often see through him at first glance.

Maria Fernanda gabs to them in three languages. With the exception of the aunt, the women smile at him and the men stand and shake hands.

Maria Fernanda says, "Refugees all of them, Harry. This is why I could never show you where I live."

"That's an insult, Maria Fernanda. I'm on your side."

"I know and I meant no insult, Harry. A slip of the lip when drinking. It happens."

"Yeah, well."

"If you're captured and tortured."

"I'd hold out to the very end," Harry says, convincing neither Maria Fernanda nor himself.

"Nobody here can afford to escape on the Clipper, but we work with people at the docks to get them on the ships. There are swindlers selling fake tickets on steamers that do not exist. My guests are very vulnerable."

Maria Fernanda takes Harry to a private room and serves him a bottle of beer from an ice box. It's not a bedroom, but it has nice furniture, overstuffed chairs and a couch that's a genuine couch, not some lousy excuse for one designed by a Victorian eunuch, a sadistic fiend who may've been Jack the Ripper.

They sit together on the couch and things soon become romantic, one thing leading to another.

As they rotate from vertical to horizontal, she takes a deep breath, sits up, and glares at him.

"What am I smelling?"

Goddamnit, she smells perfume on him. Dorothy's. These women and their sensitive noses.

"Huh? I don't smell anything," he says.

"That is not my perfume on you."

Although he knows the game is lost, Harry tugs on his shirt and sniffs. He keeps his clothes in her closet and sleeps in her bed, thinking impure thoughts.

"Perfume? What perfume?"

"Yes, Harry. Perfume. A woman's perfume."

"There's no woman in the world for me except you, Maria Fernanda."

"Liar!"

"I swear on a stack of Bibles, I'd never lie to you," Harry lies.

"Liar, liar, liar."

"Okay, okay. An American lady tourist and I crossed paths. An older, homely gal from our neighborhood in Seattle. She wore perfume strong enough to kill mosquitoes. We hugged. That's all. It's an old American custom, how you say hello."

Maria Fernanda is standing by the door. "The truth is at last escaping even though you are not telling it."

"Nothing happened," he whines. "One hug and that was it."

"Harry, I am a one-man woman. I do not expect you to be chaste, but you come to me right after being with another woman, that is a slap in the face. This is how you treat a whore!"

He goes on the counterattack. "Yeah? How about you and Peter? I am a one-woman man, faithful to you and only you, and I catch you and him holding hands, about to kiss. Put that in your pipe and smoke it."

"I do not smoke pipes or cigarettes. You and your nonsense."

"It's an expression. Slang. Don't change the subject."

"Peter and I, we were innocent and you know it. I thought he explained it to you, that I was consoling him. The PVDE had tormented him to the very edge of death after they kidnapped him out of the Canção. He is gone now, somewhere, without saying goodbye to me. Is that how lovers are to each other?"

If Harry can believe her, and he really wants to, she doesn't know Peter's fate. Best to leave it out of the conversation.

"But I didn't come to the Canção and to here with plans for you. I came there for a quiet beer or two or five. I had given up hope you'd be there. I was elated when you asked me to come with you to your home, to see it for the first time."

"You come here to satisfy curiosity and not for me? You no longer care!"

Harry is stumped. He opts to keep quiet rather than say the wrong thing, which he'd do, no matter what he says.

Maria Fernanda tells Harry to please lock the front door as he leaves and take the taxi that has been outside waiting.

Harry sighs into his beer, then obeys, double-checking that the door is locked behind him.

CHAPTER 33

By the end of the day, Harry is back in the Hotel Metropole suite. God, it's so lonely in here, it could be a cave in Antarctica. He misses Dorothy achingly. And Maria Fernanda.

Surprisingly, David too. A lecture from him would break the silence.

There's nothing left for Harry in Lisbon but trouble piled on trouble. By now, in this town where anything's possible, it isn't impossible to think that the three bodies will eventually be discovered.

Each has a connection to Horatio Alger (Harry) Antonelli. A common denominator, math-whiz Dorothy Booth might say. Harry lacks the means and connections to buy, beg, borrow or steal an alibi for any of them, let alone all three.

A nutless son of a Nazi major general remains nutless too—no fatherhood for the Fatherland forthcoming from him—an additional complication. If the Nazis roll into Lisbon, it means a firing squad for Harry, a citizen of neutral America or not.

Harry packs up and walks to the railway station, with no particular destination in mind. The station and its entrance is a beauty with its classical twin arches, but he has no time for architectural sightseeing.

The Hotel Palacio in Estoril sounds like a swell stopover. It's closer to the Atlantic Ocean and home, but there's no solid logic in this choice other than it's not Lisbon and he can afford to travel there.

There are no trains running there anytime soon, so he catches a bus, an hour's ride that tests the strength of Dr. Booth's fillings.

The Estoril Casino is in a word: glamorous. Five stories high and 100 meters long, it is the lap of luxury. There are swimming pools, a sprawling gambling den, and a golf course the Duke of Windsor is said to frequently enjoy.

Hmm, if they're still around and if Harry happens to bump into the Duchess while the Duke's off golfing, and she's pissed off about him playing golf all the time and bored, and she takes him up on the offer of a drink... The Brits, they all drink gin, even an American married to one, he assumes, so after he slips a couple of dry martinis into her—

Stop it, Harry tells himself. Him and that skinny dame having a drunken afternoon roll on silk sheets is as likely as him taking on the powers of Flash Gordon, Batman, Captain Marvel, and Dick Tracy. With or without a cape and a wrist radio.

Harry asks at the desk for a room. There are no vacancies and Harry isn't sure if he wants one anyway, not at these prices, even stiffer than the Metropole's $8 a day. The weather's fine; he can sleep under a tree.

With the rest of his dough, he's thinking a ship or a plane to Britain or a hop across the Mediterranean to Africa, to Casablanca. Then on to the Azores, from there a flight to the States. Whichever, it has to be one of those choices and soon, before he's flat broke and his name shows up on a detention list. As far as Harry's concerned, he's as innocent as a newborn baby, but try telling that to those PVDE louses and their Nazi puppeteers.

What he'll do, if he can make it to the States, is he'll try being a good son for a change. He'll live at home and catch up with his parents and Tabby. Dorothy too if she'll cooperate. He'll find a job, even if it's high-school teaching and coaching, a nice peaceful time when he'll stop drinking and carousing, or at least cut back. The best part is, he won't be caught in the middle of a war, not in the near future anyway.

Half the geniuses in the War Department are isolationists. Sure, there's plenty of water between Europe and America, so nobody's worried much about the Nazis wading ashore on the Eastern seaboard. Harry isn't worried either. He knows what most of them don't, that there's no isotope uranium ticketed for London, let alone Washington and New York.

The Japs he's not so sure about. They're pushy and sneaky and as mean as snakes. The Pacific's big, yeah, but who knows where they are in their battleships. Hawaii's the only safe island in that ocean, thanks to all the Navy ships and that new radar invention he's read about.

Those posters he's seen of Japs with buck teeth and thick glasses, proof they're crummy aviators—he takes them with a grain of salt. Propaganda bullshit as dumb as what the Germans put out.

If Japan starts a war and one out of ten of their soldiers or pilots is like Chuck Shimizu, we'll have our hands full. But war or no war, FDR has us mobilizing, so Harry knows he'll have to eventually join up.

SPECULATIVE NOTE: Should Harry survive his extended summer in Europe and return home after Pearl Harbor, he'll arrive just in time to see Chuck and his family being carted off to the Tule Lake internment camp. Harry will make such a fuss that it'll take six Seattle Police officers to billy-club him into submission and haul him off to the pokey.

Thinking of Dorothy's Spitfire ace, as invisible as if bathed by an invisibility ray, what Harry will think about doing is signing up for the Army Air Corps. He's heard of the Flying Tigers over in China, mixing it up in the air with the Japs. If there's no war on the home front, maybe they'll train him to fly a P-40 Warhawk and send him there. Shouldn't be a problem if they don't ask too many question about what he's been doing for the last two years.

Either way, he can become a real ace for Dorothy.

Like the Metropole, the Palacio's teeming with Kraut spies and agents, so he knows he'd better keep his lips buttoned up on subjects real and fantastical.

That in mind, he strikes up a conversation with an Englishman at a bar who's drinking gin and tonic, like so many of them do. Harry shudders at the smell of gin. As far as he's concerned, the juniper berry is a toxic weed, a prime candidate for DDT.

The guy is an obvious secret agent, where every harmless statement has a question buried in it. They talk about a whole bunch of nothing, buy each other a couple of rounds, until Harry decides to get up and leave.

They shake hands and make formal introductions.

"Harry Antonelli."

"Ian Fleming. You know, Harry, you remind me of someone."

"Yeah, who?"

"That's the bloody problem. I haven't met him yet, but you're the spitting image, though you probably don't look alike and he'll be a Brit, not a Yank."

"That's all you know about him?" Harry says, thinking that the Limey can't hold his gin.

"I'm afraid so. Oh, one other thing. I hope you're not insulted. I know that he will have somewhat more *savoir faire* than you."

Harry smiles, thinking that's what gin will do to the gray matter, making your brains permanently fuzzy, even to Englishmen who grew up on it. Unlike Kentucky whiskey, which after recovering from your hangover, you'll be as fit as a fiddle.

He says, "Most people have more polish and tact than I do, so no offense taken. If you ever do cross paths with this figment of your imagination, be sure to say hello."

"One other small note," Fleming says. "He'll have a license to kill."

Harry tenses. Is he being set up for a Horst Wessel confession? Pinning Peter and Dieter on him too?

"You're turning green, mate. Are you all right?"

Harry stares at the backbar.

"He'll be fictional if that's what's bothering you."

"Like in a novel?"

"That's a smashing idea, Harry."

Harry stands and gives the Fleming guy a quick salute. "I'm liking your character now. Good luck, Ian. Don't take any wooden nickels."

CHAPTER 34

A dolf Hitler's office is a monument within a monument. The Reich Chancellery, designed by Albert Speer, Hitler's architect, was completed in 1939, a stern assemblage of marble and granite, its grand entry flanked by pillars.

It is meant to intimidate and it does.

HISTORICAL NOTE: The original Chancellery was built in 1871 for Otto von Bismarck. Hitler deemed it "fit for a soap factory." Cost of its replacement was 90 million Reichsmarks, the equivalent of $1 billion today. By 1945, it had been bombed into rubble. What remained upright was demolished by the Soviets.

Hitler's private office occupies 400 square meters and is two stories tall. It serves well for the man who intends to be the most powerful leader in history.

Reinhard Heydrich stands like a statue in that office before his *Führer*, his arms and legs tightly together so his trembling will not show.

"As you have ordered, *mein Führer*, I am reporting on my trip to Lisbon."

Hitler studies a man who is more black and blue than Nordic white.

"What happened to your face, Reinhard?"

Heydrich has stalled giving his report as long as he can.

"I was careless and walked into an opening door."

"It must have been a large door."

"It was, *mein Führer*, made of steel."

"You must stop the drinking, Reinhard."

The SS *Obergrupperführer* studies his boots, feigning contrition. "I will, I promise. I shamefully admit, it was the schnapps that made me clumsy."

Once explained, a lie or the truth, the man's damaged face is of no further interest to Adolf Hitler.

"This Lisbon project of yours?"

"It is progressing swimmingly."

Report of the closure will not be made, officially or unofficially, to Berlin. The PVDE is embarrassed, as they should be, and are keeping a lid on it. Failure does not exist, it cannot. When eventually cornered, Heydrich will devise an excuse, blaming everyone and everything imaginable except himself.

He thinks of the American incessantly, of how to capture him and personally skin him, one square centimeter of flesh at a time. Because of the debacle at the uranium plant, he is helpless to act now.

"You have recommended that we invade Portugal immediately," Hitler says. "Is this in connection to the secret weapon project?"

"Yes. We can set up camps and have ample slave labor for—"

Hitler lifts a hand. "No. We will take the Iberian Peninsula in geographical order. I continue to press Franco to join the war. He is weakening. It will not be long. A month or two. Then Salazar will have to fall into line. Leave political speculation to me, Reinhard."

"Yes, *mein Führer.*"

"Your schedule for this uranium substance, how long?"

"There are minor technical problems that will be corrected very soon, *mein Führer.*"

Reinhard isn't looking him in the eye. He is concealing trouble. Mad science, Hitler muses. He is very skeptical. He has been promised dazzling weapons before, but nothing is delivered except promises. Willy Messerschmitt and his jet turbine airplane that will fly circles around Spitfires. Wernher von Braun and his rockets at Peenemünde that cannot be defended by the enemy.

Hitler is out of patience with fairy tales and secret gadgetry. He has Operation Sea Lion to plan. Then the Bolsheviks, Stalin's head delivered to him on a stick.

"That is good," Hitler says, returning to the papers and maps on his desk, in essence dismissing Heydrich.

The heels of Heydrich's boots click together. *"Heil Hitler."*

He departs, already devising excuses. Jews and Communists can be blamed. He knows that the invasion of England and the Soviet Union is on Hitler's mind constantly. Failure in Lisbon will merely provide another justification to dispose of the Russians.

*****

Alone again with his thoughts, Hitler takes from a locked desk drawer the sketch of a radiation-poisoned Winston Churchill.

Taking deep breaths, he studies it with moist hands.

After London falls and Churchill is captured and brought to him, he will have no need for magic powder. Hitler has heard of a promising young doctor named Josef Mengele, a man with a zest for human experimentation, innovation. He will have Dr. Mengele work on Churchill; he can do magical things to the *Engländer* without uranium.

Hitler notifies his secretary that he isn't seeing visitors until further notice and takes the sketch into a bathroom.

EPILOGUE

What a difference 77 years makes.

Spam™ was a canned lunchmeat then, not annoying messages on computers, which hadn't been invented yet. Static cling hadn't been cured and there were no Klingons. You could buy a 1940 Pontiac for $875. Now, you can't find a new one at any price.

During the summer of 1940, the streets of Lisbon were clogged with refugees fleeing Hitler. In their company was a collection of spies, double agents, and triple agents. Portugal was neutral and money spoke louder than ideology.

Dusko Popov, one such triple agent, said, "Lisbon was an *Alice in Wonderland* experience, passing from one world to another, except in this case both worlds were abnormal."

Nowadays, tourists clog the streets. They're mostly Europeans, with a smattering of Americans. The only agents around and about are travel agents.

Some things have changed while not changing. Take the building on the corner of Rua do Carmo and Rua Garrett in the city's Chiado area. There have been external modifications; the windows are different and they have awnings. And the corner lamppost is gone.

The real transformation is inside. During World War Two, it was a German propaganda bookstore. These days, it markets home coffee-making equipment and supplies.

Copies of *Mein Kampf* were stacked on the shelves then, espresso machines now. Then, poisonous Nazi dogma was sold. The means to brew excellent coffee is offered now.

G.A.

2017

ABOUT THE AUTHOR

Gary Alexander is the author of sixteen novels. *Disappeared*, first in the Buster Hightower series, has been optioned to Universal Studios.

He's also written 150+ short stories and sold travel articles to six major dailies.

One story appeared in *Best American Mystery Stories 2010*, and another in *Mystery Writers of America Presents Ice Cold: Tales of Intrigue from the Cold War* anthology.

On his last visit to Lisbon in 2015, Alexander walked where Harry Antonelli had in 1940, although somewhat less recklessly.

His website is www.garyralexander.net